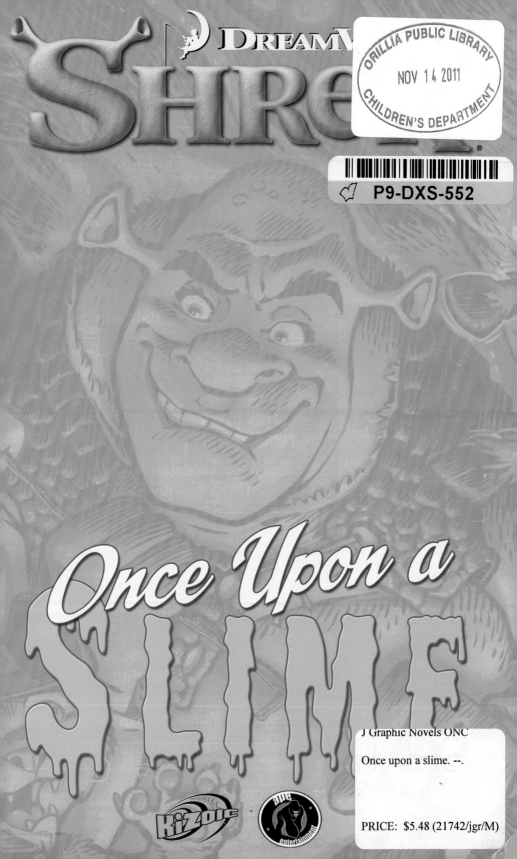

DREAMWORKS SHREK®

Once Upon a SLIME

KIZOIC

ape entertainment

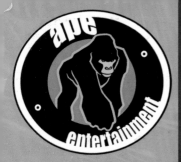

APE ENTERTAINMENT

David Hedgecock
Co-Publisher / General Partner
DHedgecock@Ape-Entertainment.com

Brent E. Erwin
Co-Publisher / General Partner
BErwin@Ape-Entertainment.com

Jason M. Burns
Editor-in-Chief
JBurns@Ape-Entertainment.com

Kevin Freeman
Managing Editor
KFreeman@Ape-Entertainment.com

Matt Anderson
Assistant Editor
MAnderson@Ape-Entertainment.com

Troy Dye
Submissions Editor
TDye@Ape-Entertainment.com

Steve Bryant
Designer
SBryant@Ape-Entertainment.com

Ape Entertainment
P.O. Box 7100
San Diego, CA 92167
www.ApeComics.com

APE DIGITAL COMIC SITE:
Apecmx.com

TWITTER:
Twitter.com/ApeComics

FACEBOOK:
Facebook.com/pages/Ape-Entertainment

MYSPACE:
MySpace.com/ApeEntertainment

To find more great DreamWorks Animation comics, visit us on the web at Kizoic.com

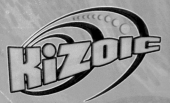

Golden Goose...Egg!

Written by:
Arie Kaplan
w/Jason M. Burns

Pencils, Inks & Tones by:
Christine Larsen

Colors by:
Tim Durning

Fairy Berry Fever

Written by:
Kevin Freeman

Pencils & Inks by:
Drew Rausch

Colors by:
Matt Kaufenberg

Buddies Night Out

Written by:
Troy Dye &
Tom Kelesides

Pencils, Inks & Tones by:
Christine Larsen

Colors by:
Tim Durning

Dentist for the Dronkeys

Written by:
Jim Hankins

Pencils & Inks by:
Rob Reilly

Colors by:
Tim Durning

Cover by: Robb Mommaerts & Rolando Mallad

Letters by: Chris Studabaker

Published by Ape Entertainment L.L.C., San Diego, CA (www.ApeComics.com).
Proudly printed in the USA.

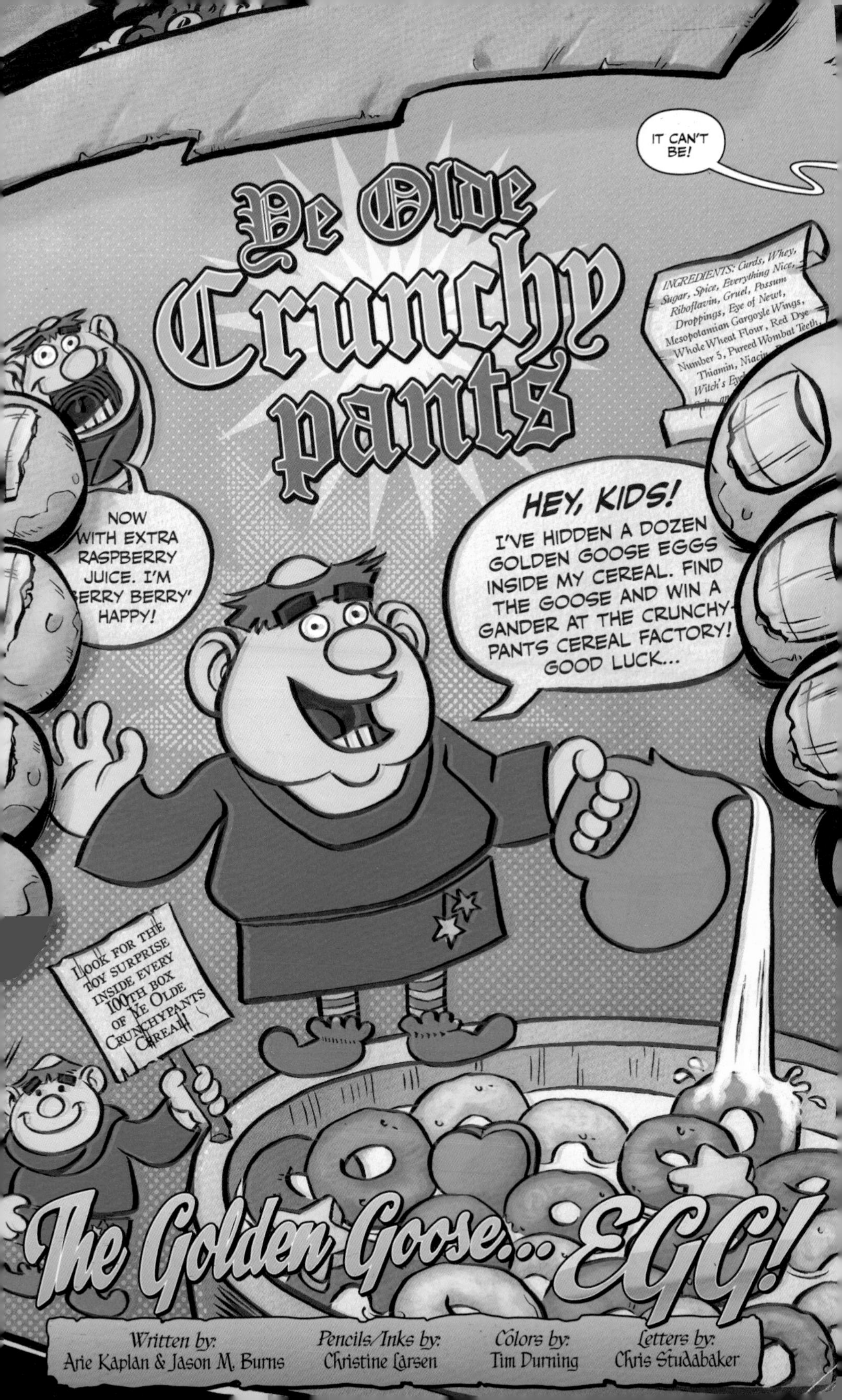
IT CAN'T BE!
Ye Olde Crunchy pants
INGREDIENTS: Curds, Whey, Sugar, Spice, Everything Nice, Riboflavin, Gruel, Possum Droppings, Eye of Newt, Mesopotamian Gargoyle Wings, Whole Wheat Flour, Red Dye Number 5, Pureed Wombat Teeth, Thiamin, Witch's
NOW WITH EXTRA RASPBERRY JUICE. I'M 'BERRY BERRY' HAPPY!
HEY, KIDS! I'VE HIDDEN A DOZEN GOLDEN GOOSE EGGS INSIDE MY CEREAL. FIND THE GOOSE AND WIN A GANDER AT THE CRUNCHY-PANTS CEREAL FACTORY! GOOD LUCK...
LOOK FOR THE TOY SURPRISE INSIDE EVERY 100TH BOX OF YE OLDE CRUNCHYPANTS CEREAL!
The Golden Goose... EGG!
Written by: Arie Kaplan & Jason M. Burns
Pencils/Inks by: Christine Larsen
Colors by: Tim Durning
Letters by: Chris Studabaker

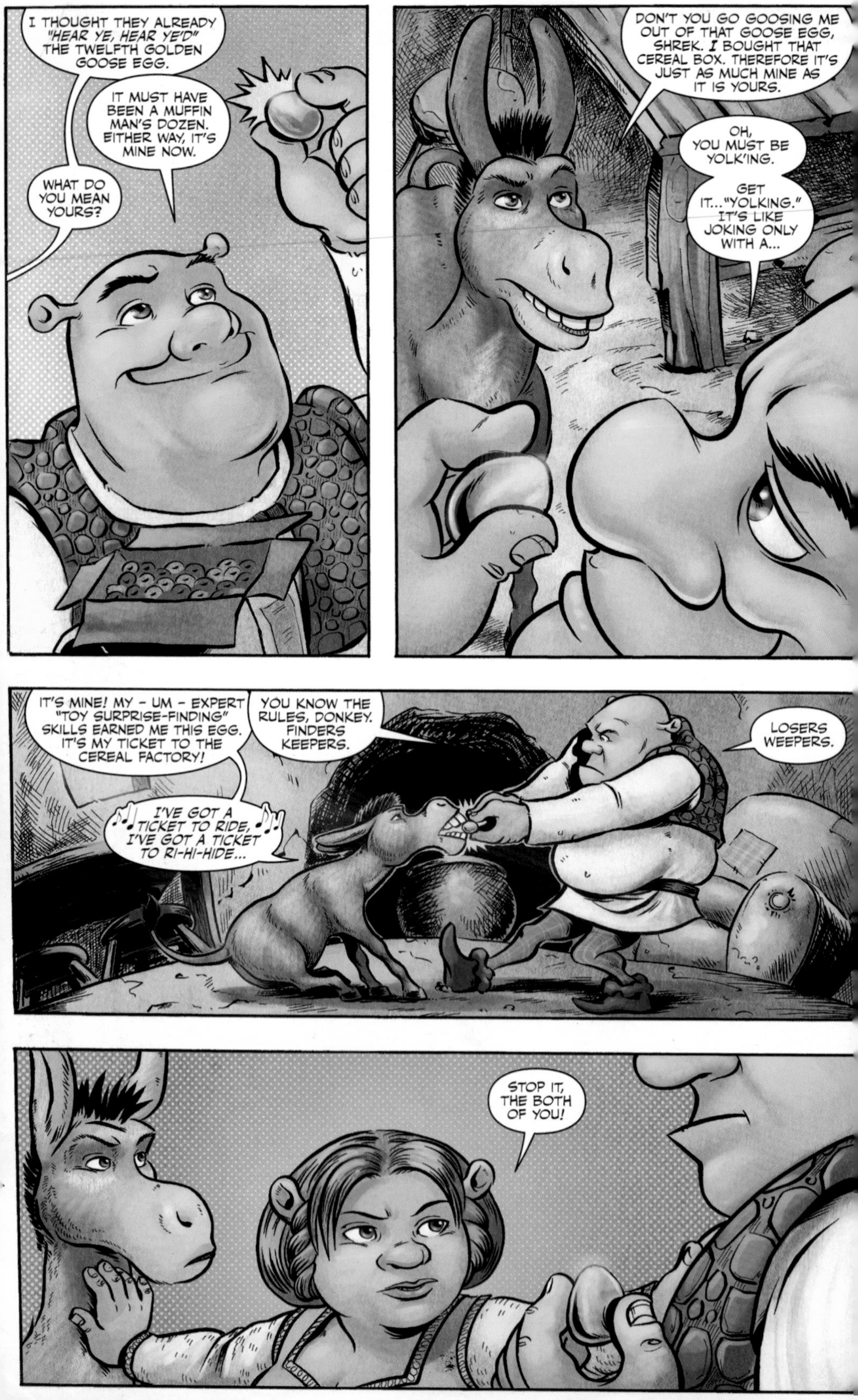
I THOUGHT THEY ALREADY "HEAR YE, HEAR YE'D" THE TWELFTH GOLDEN GOOSE EGG.
IT MUST HAVE BEEN A MUFFIN MAN'S DOZEN. EITHER WAY, IT'S MINE NOW.
WHAT DO YOU MEAN YOURS?
DON'T YOU GO GOOSING ME OUT OF THAT GOOSE EGG, SHREK. I BOUGHT THAT CEREAL BOX. THEREFORE IT'S JUST AS MUCH MINE AS IT IS YOURS.
OH, YOU MUST BE YOLK'ING.
GET IT..."YOLKING." IT'S LIKE JOKING ONLY WITH A...
IT'S MINE! MY - UM - EXPERT "TOY SURPRISE-FINDING" SKILLS EARNED ME THIS EGG. IT'S MY TICKET TO THE CEREAL FACTORY!
YOU KNOW THE RULES, DONKEY. FINDERS KEEPERS.
LOSERS WEEPERS.
I'VE GOT A TICKET TO RIDE, I'VE GOT A TICKET TO RI-HI-HIDE...
STOP IT, THE BOTH OF YOU!

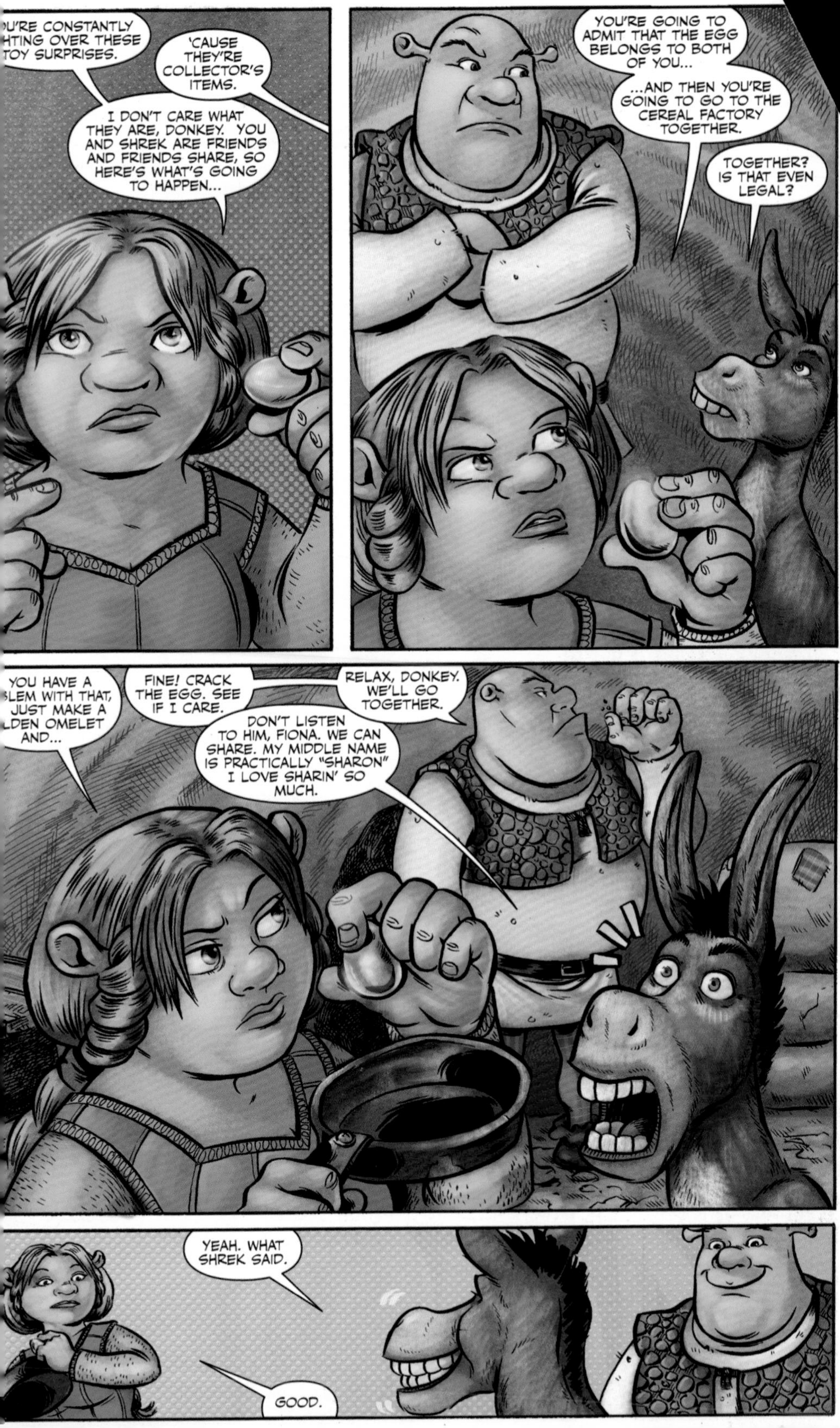
U'RE CONSTANTLY HTING OVER THESE TOY SURPRISES.
'CAUSE THEY'RE COLLECTOR'S ITEMS.
I DON'T CARE WHAT THEY ARE, DONKEY. YOU AND SHREK ARE FRIENDS AND FRIENDS SHARE, SO HERE'S WHAT'S GOING TO HAPPEN...
YOU'RE GOING TO ADMIT THAT THE EGG BELONGS TO BOTH OF YOU...
...AND THEN YOU'RE GOING TO GO TO THE CEREAL FACTORY TOGETHER.
TOGETHER? IS THAT EVEN LEGAL?
YOU HAVE A BLEM WITH THAT, JUST MAKE A LDEN OMELET AND...
FINE! CRACK THE EGG. SEE IF I CARE.
RELAX, DONKEY. WE'LL GO TOGETHER.
DON'T LISTEN TO HIM, FIONA. WE CAN SHARE. MY MIDDLE NAME IS PRACTICALLY "SHARON" I LOVE SHARIN' SO MUCH.
YEAH. WHAT SHREK SAID.
GOOD.

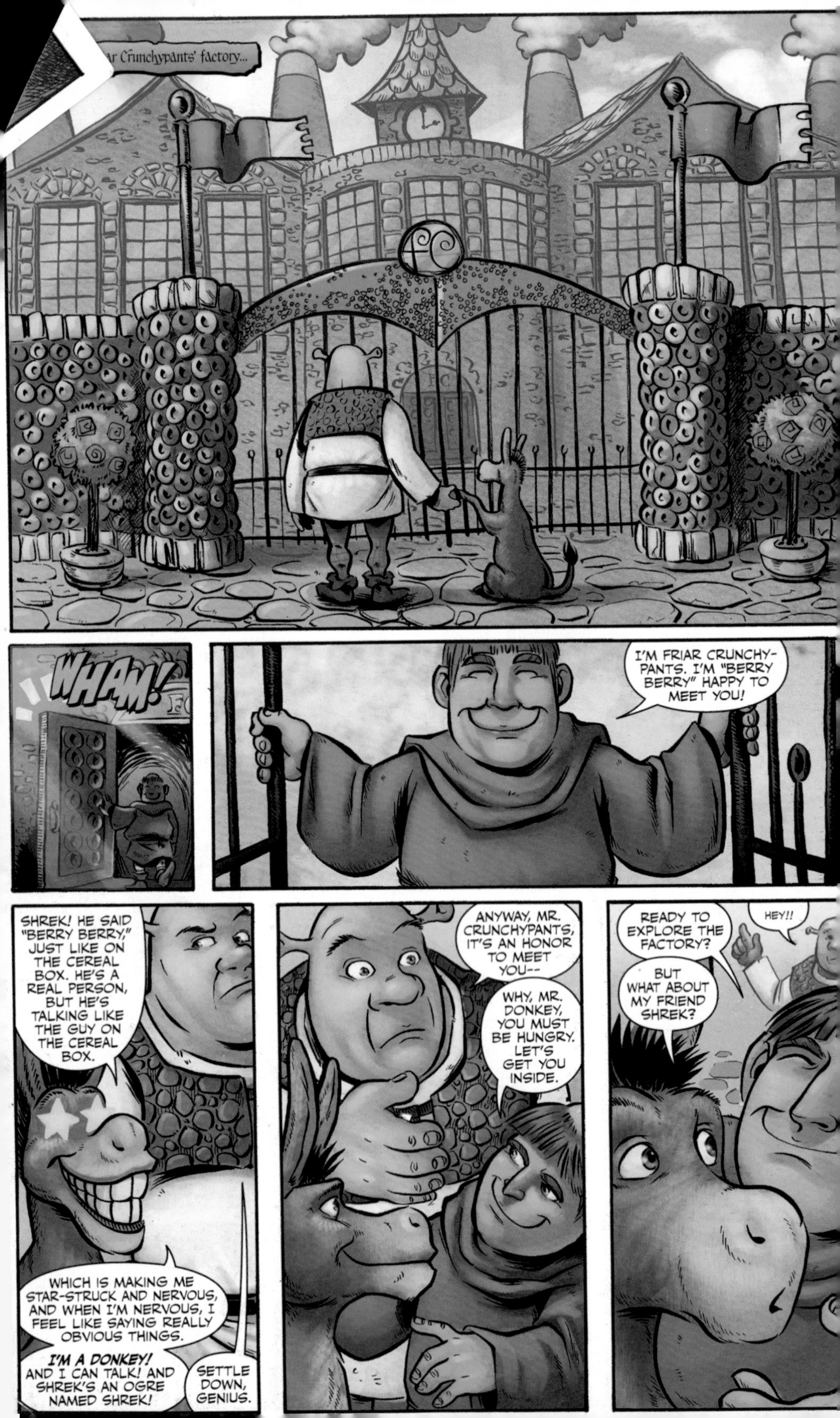
...ar Crunchypants' factory...
WHAM!
I'M FRIAR CRUNCHY-PANTS. I'M "BERRY BERRY" HAPPY TO MEET YOU!
SHREK! HE SAID "BERRY BERRY," JUST LIKE ON THE CEREAL BOX. HE'S A REAL PERSON, BUT HE'S TALKING LIKE THE GUY ON THE CEREAL BOX.
WHICH IS MAKING ME STAR-STRUCK AND NERVOUS, AND WHEN I'M NERVOUS, I FEEL LIKE SAYING REALLY OBVIOUS THINGS.
I'M A DONKEY! AND I CAN TALK! AND SHREK'S AN OGRE NAMED SHREK!
SETTLE DOWN, GENIUS.
ANYWAY, MR. CRUNCHYPANTS, IT'S AN HONOR TO MEET YOU--
WHY, MR. DONKEY, YOU MUST BE HUNGRY. LET'S GET YOU INSIDE.
READY TO EXPLORE THE FACTORY?
HEY!!
BUT WHAT ABOUT MY FRIEND SHREK?

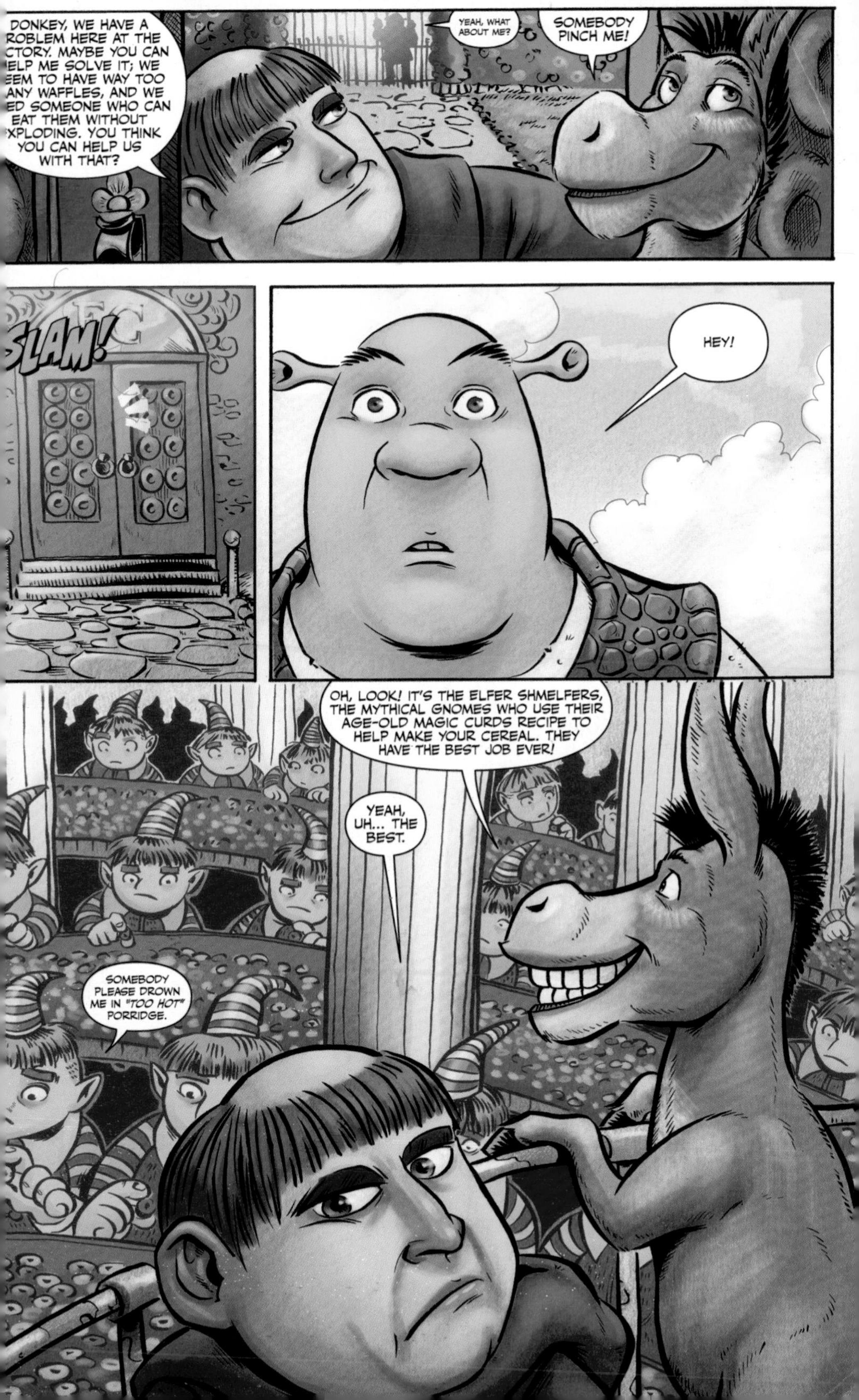
DONKEY, WE HAVE A
ROBLEM HERE AT THE
CTORY. MAYBE YOU CAN
ELP ME SOLVE IT; WE
EEM TO HAVE WAY TOO
ANY WAFFLES, AND WE
ED SOMEONE WHO CAN
EAT THEM WITHOUT
XPLODING. YOU THINK
YOU CAN HELP US
WITH THAT?
YEAH, WHAT ABOUT ME?
SOMEBODY PINCH ME!
SLAM!
HEY!
OH, LOOK! IT'S THE ELFER SHMELFERS, THE MYTHICAL GNOMES WHO USE THEIR AGE-OLD MAGIC CURDS RECIPE TO HELP MAKE YOUR CEREAL. THEY HAVE THE BEST JOB EVER!
YEAH, UH... THE BEST.
SOMEBODY PLEASE DROWN ME IN "TOO HOT" PORRIDGE.

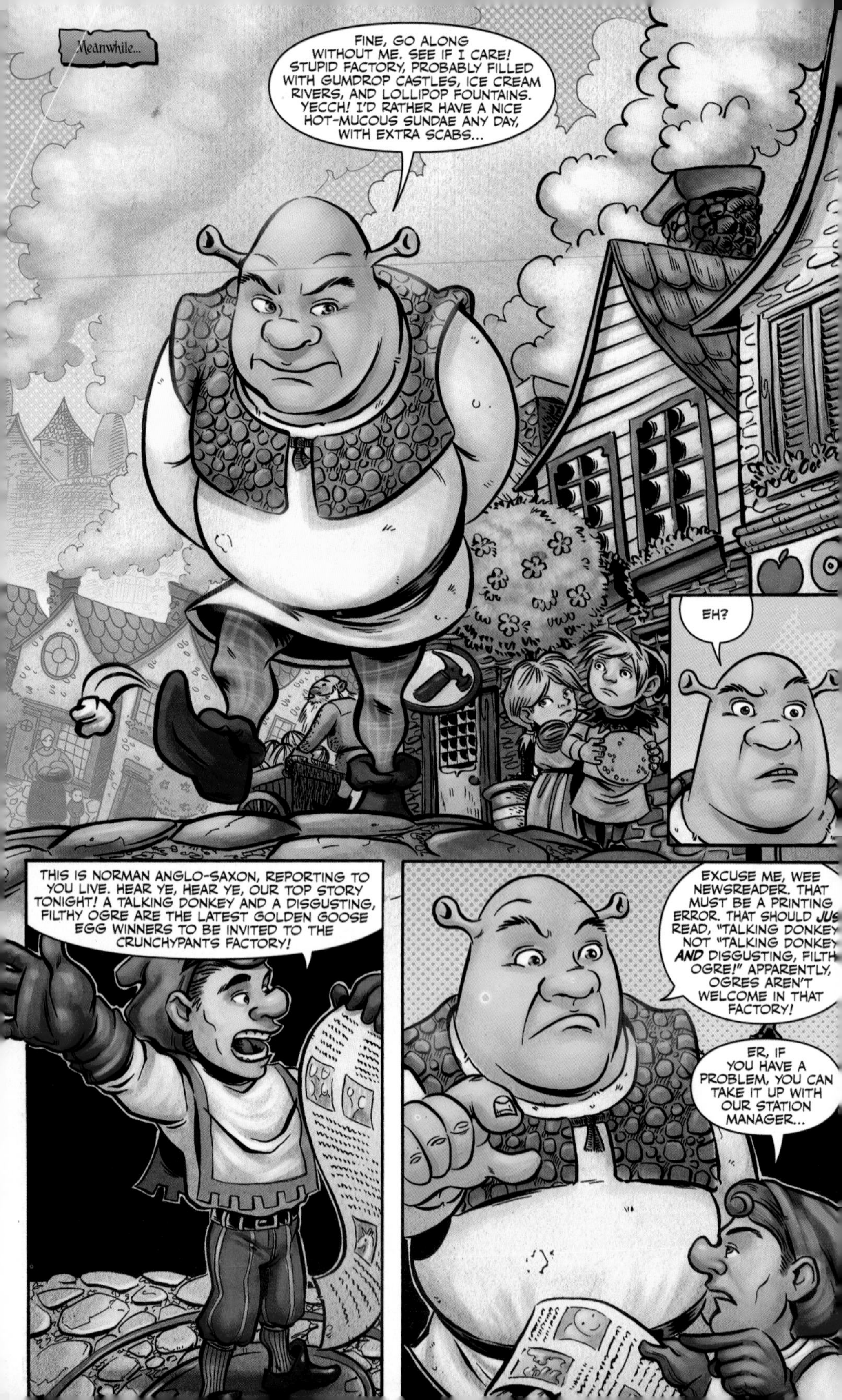
Meanwhile...
FINE, GO ALONG WITHOUT ME. SEE IF I CARE! STUPID FACTORY, PROBABLY FILLED WITH GUMDROP CASTLES, ICE CREAM RIVERS, AND LOLLIPOP FOUNTAINS. YECCH! I'D RATHER HAVE A NICE HOT-MUCOUS SUNDAE ANY DAY, WITH EXTRA SCABS...
EH?
THIS IS NORMAN ANGLO-SAXON, REPORTING TO YOU LIVE. HEAR YE, HEAR YE, OUR TOP STORY TONIGHT! A TALKING DONKEY AND A DISGUSTING, FILTHY OGRE ARE THE LATEST GOLDEN GOOSE EGG WINNERS TO BE INVITED TO THE CRUNCHYPANTS FACTORY!
EXCUSE ME, WEE NEWSREADER. THAT MUST BE A PRINTING ERROR. THAT SHOULD JUS READ, "TALKING DONKEY NOT "TALKING DONKEY AND DISGUSTING, FILTH OGRE!" APPARENTLY, OGRES AREN'T WELCOME IN THAT FACTORY!
ER, IF YOU HAVE A PROBLEM, YOU CAN TAKE IT UP WITH OUR STATION MANAGER...

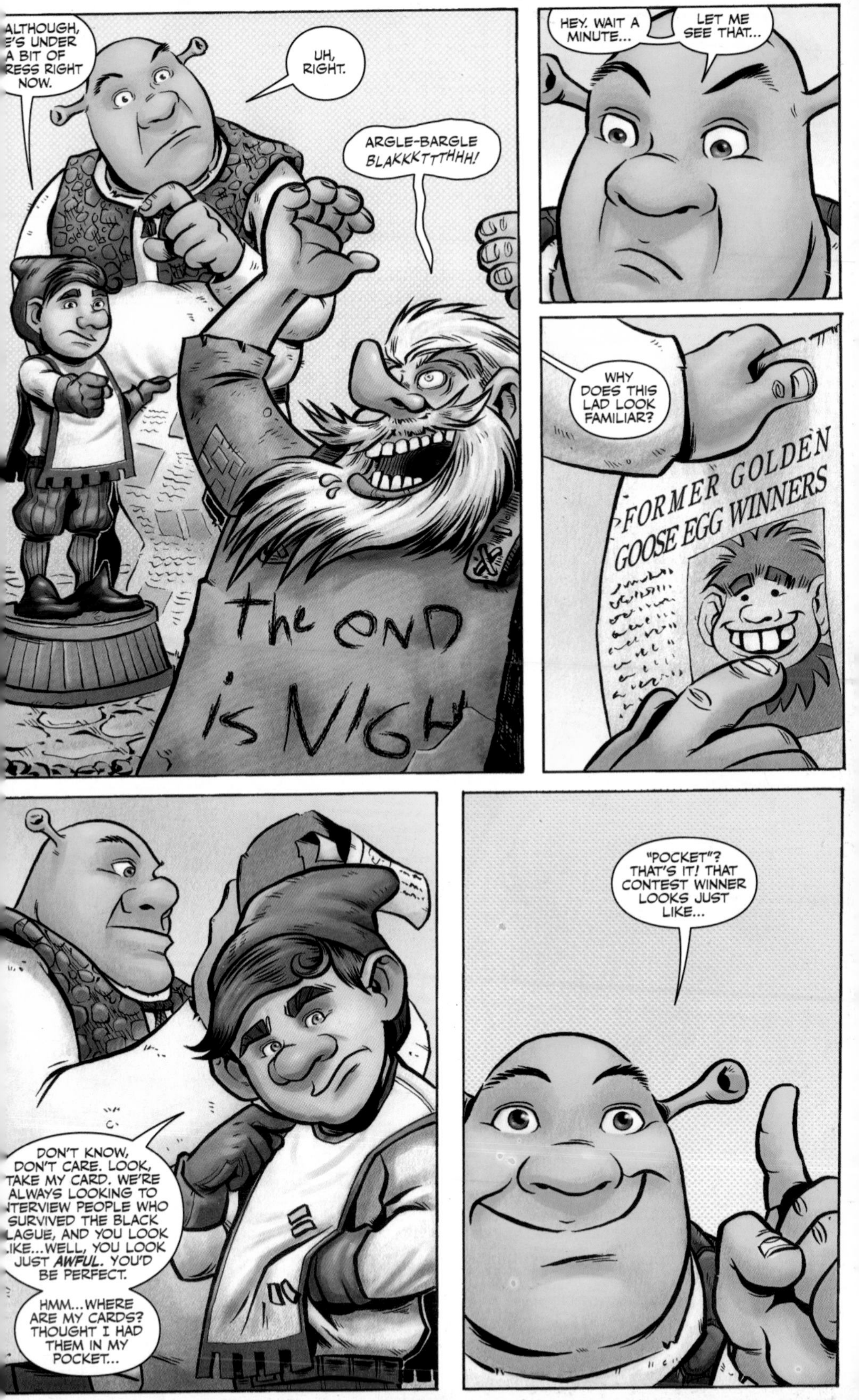
ALTHOUGH, E'S UNDER A BIT OF RESS RIGHT NOW.
UH, RIGHT.
ARGLE-BARGLE BLAKKKTTTHHH!
the END is NIGH
HEY. WAIT A MINUTE...
LET ME SEE THAT...
WHY DOES THIS LAD LOOK FAMILIAR?
FORMER GOLDEN GOOSE EGG WINNERS
DON'T KNOW, DON'T CARE. LOOK, TAKE MY CARD. WE'RE ALWAYS LOOKING TO ITERVIEW PEOPLE WHO SURVIVED THE BLACK LAGUE, AND YOU LOOK LIKE...WELL, YOU LOOK JUST AWFUL. YOU'D BE PERFECT.
HMM...WHERE ARE MY CARDS? THOUGHT I HAD THEM IN MY POCKET...
"POCKET"? THAT'S IT! THAT CONTEST WINNER LOOKS JUST LIKE...

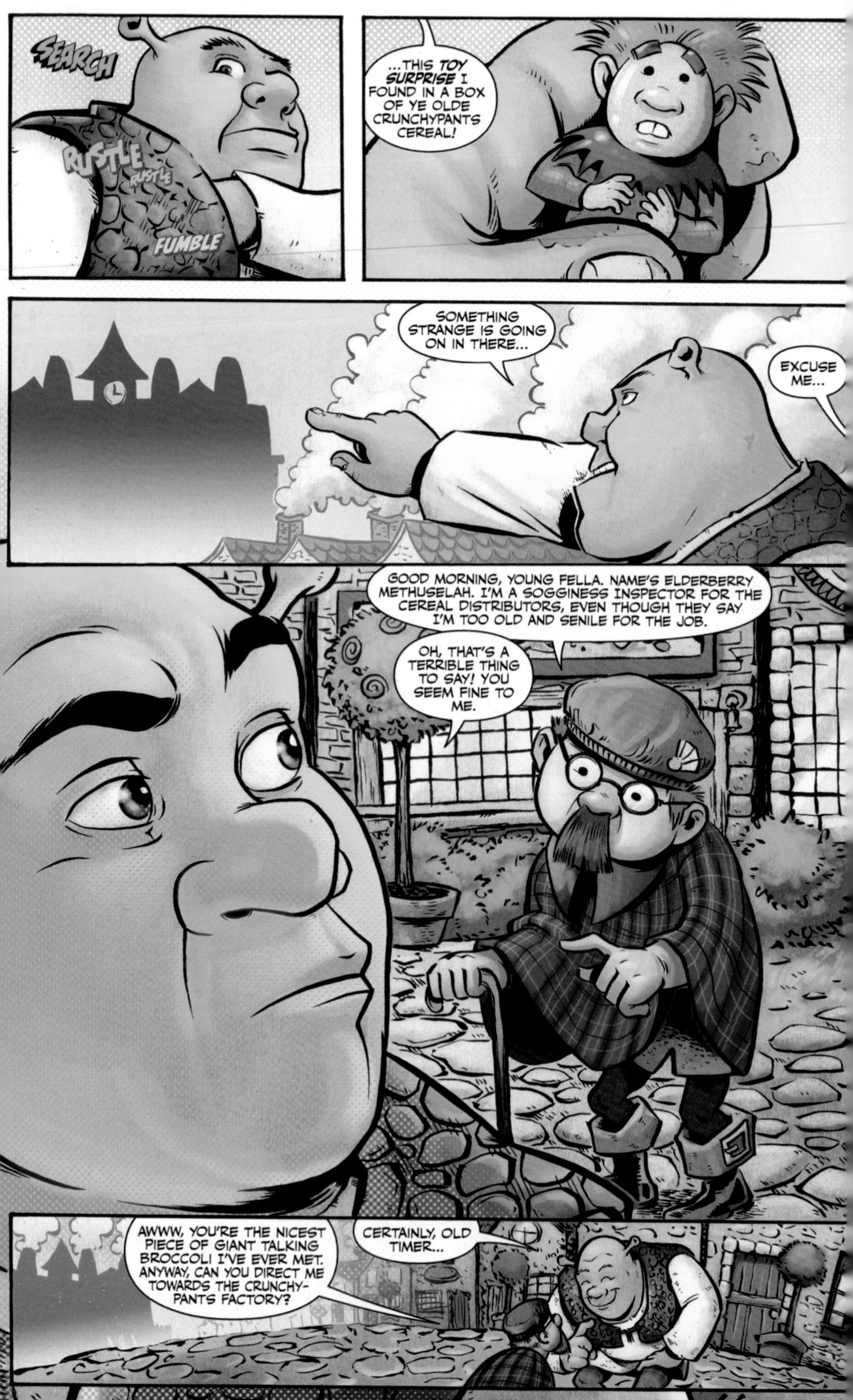
SEARCH
RUSTLE
RUSTLE
FUMBLE
...THIS TOY SURPRISE I FOUND IN A BOX OF YE OLDE CRUNCHYPANTS CEREAL!
SOMETHING STRANGE IS GOING ON IN THERE...
EXCUSE ME...
GOOD MORNING, YOUNG FELLA. NAME'S ELDERBERRY METHUSELAH. I'M A SOGGINESS INSPECTOR FOR THE CEREAL DISTRIBUTORS, EVEN THOUGH THEY SAY I'M TOO OLD AND SENILE FOR THE JOB.
OH, THAT'S A TERRIBLE THING TO SAY! YOU SEEM FINE TO ME.
AWWW, YOU'RE THE NICEST PIECE OF GIANT TALKING BROCCOLI I'VE EVER MET. ANYWAY, CAN YOU DIRECT ME TOWARDS THE CRUNCHY-PANTS FACTORY?
CERTAINLY, OLD TIMER...

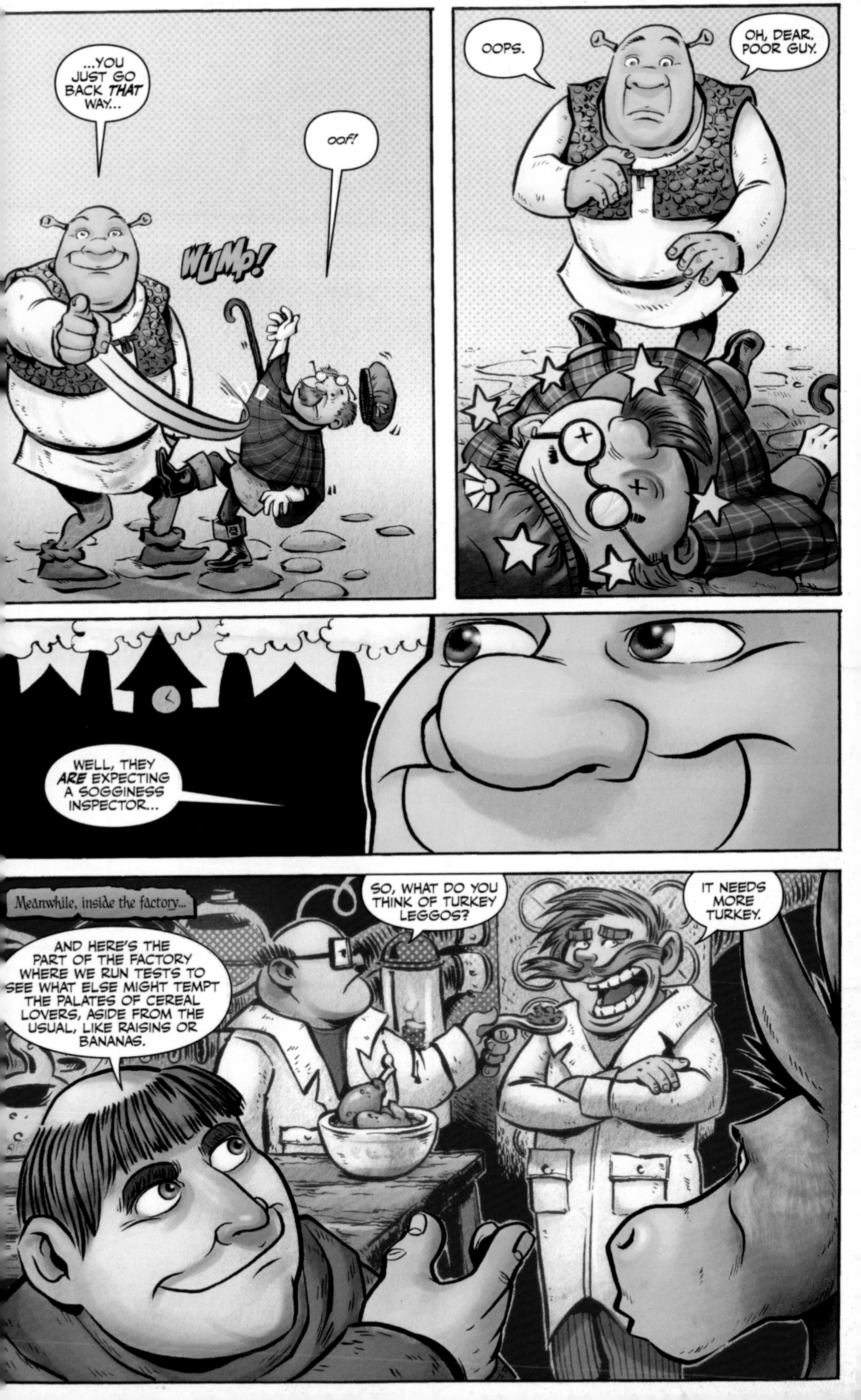

...YOU JUST GO BACK *THAT* WAY...
oof!
WUMP!
OOPS.
OH, DEAR. POOR GUY.
WELL, THEY *ARE* EXPECTING A SOGGINESS INSPECTOR...
Meanwhile, inside the factory...
AND HERE'S THE PART OF THE FACTORY WHERE WE RUN TESTS TO SEE WHAT ELSE MIGHT TEMPT THE PALATES OF CEREAL LOVERS, ASIDE FROM THE USUAL, LIKE RAISINS OR BANANAS.
SO, WHAT DO YOU THINK OF TURKEY LEGGOS?
IT NEEDS MORE TURKEY.

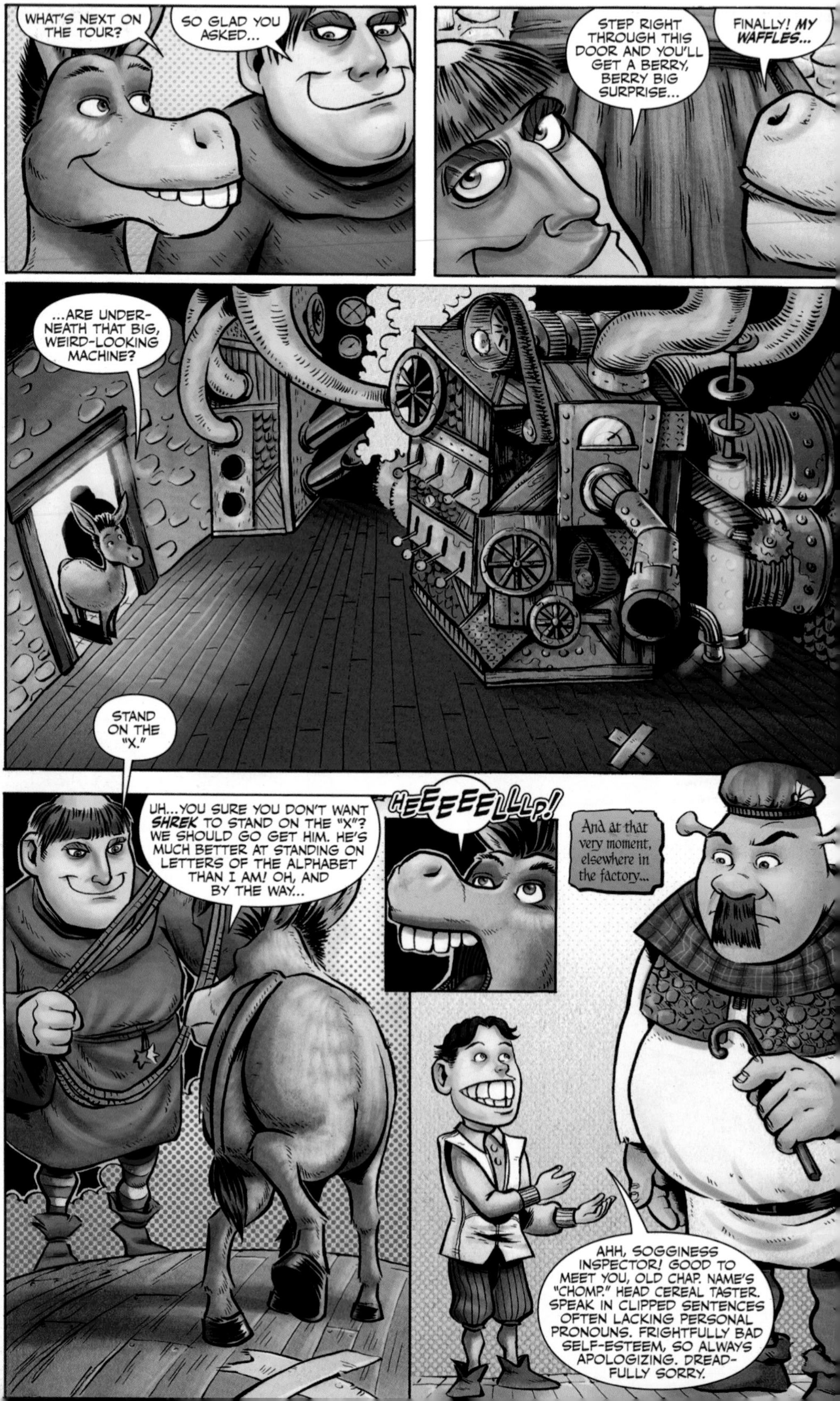

WHAT'S NEXT ON THE TOUR?
SO GLAD YOU ASKED...
STEP RIGHT THROUGH THIS DOOR AND YOU'LL GET A BERRY, BERRY BIG SURPRISE...
FINALLY! MY WAFFLES...
...ARE UNDER-NEATH THAT BIG, WEIRD-LOOKING MACHINE?
STAND ON THE "X."
UH...YOU SURE YOU DON'T WANT SHREK TO STAND ON THE "X"? WE SHOULD GO GET HIM. HE'S MUCH BETTER AT STANDING ON LETTERS OF THE ALPHABET THAN I AM! OH, AND BY THE WAY...
HEEEEEELLLLP!
And at that very moment, elsewhere in the factory...
AHH, SOGGINESS INSPECTOR! GOOD TO MEET YOU, OLD CHAP. NAME'S "CHOMP." HEAD CEREAL TASTER. SPEAK IN CLIPPED SENTENCES OFTEN LACKING PERSONAL PRONOUNS. FRIGHTFULLY BAD SELF-ESTEEM, SO ALWAYS APOLOGIZING. DREAD-FULLY SORRY.

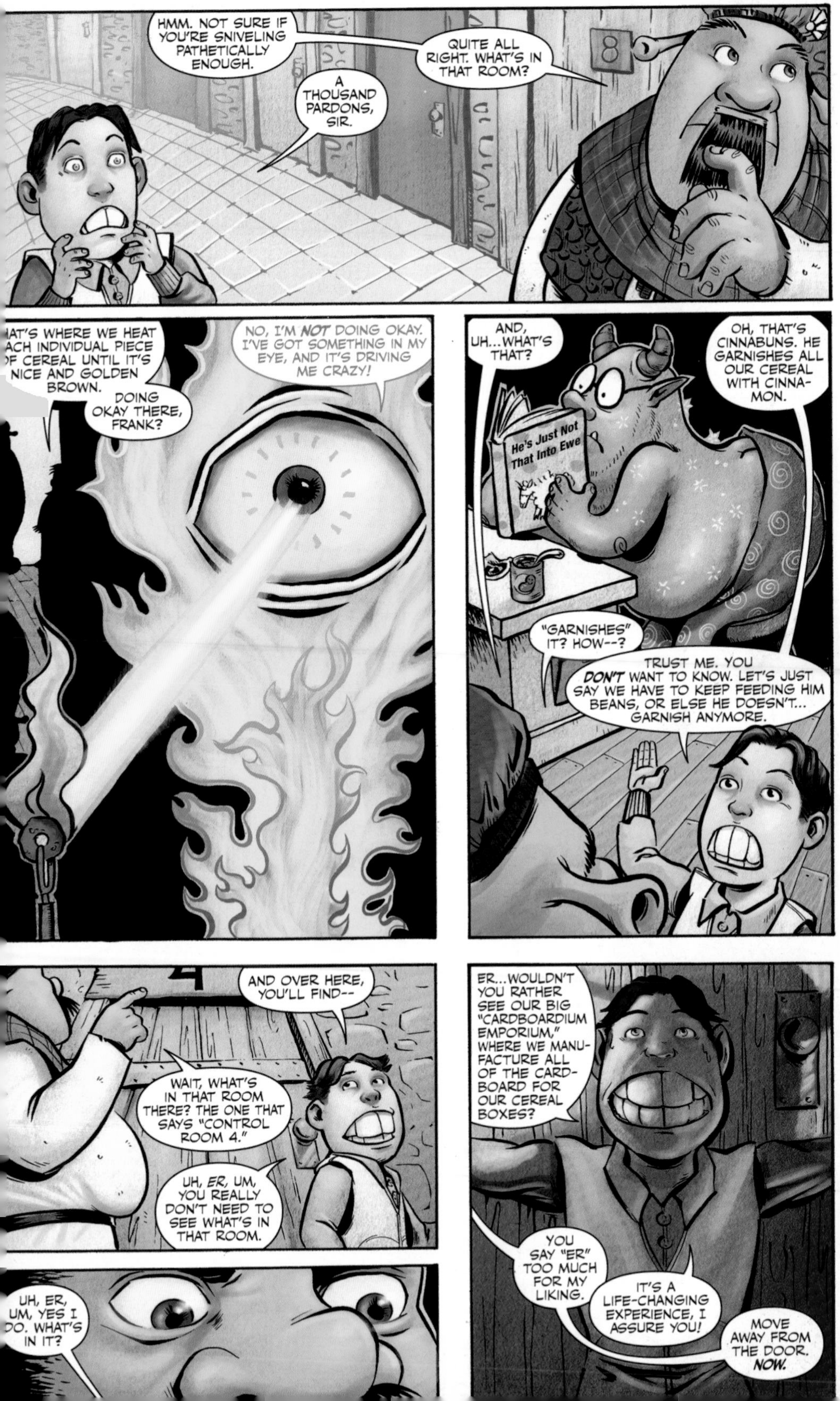

HMM. NOT SURE IF YOU'RE SNIVELING PATHETICALLY ENOUGH.
A THOUSAND PARDONS, SIR.
QUITE ALL RIGHT. WHAT'S IN THAT ROOM?
8
AT'S WHERE WE HEAT ACH INDIVIDUAL PIECE F CEREAL UNTIL IT'S NICE AND GOLDEN BROWN.
DOING OKAY THERE, FRANK?
NO, I'M NOT DOING OKAY. I'VE GOT SOMETHING IN MY EYE, AND IT'S DRIVING ME CRAZY!
AND, UH...WHAT'S THAT?
OH, THAT'S CINNABUNS. HE GARNISHES ALL OUR CEREAL WITH CINNAMON.
He's Just Not That Into Ewe
"GARNISHES" IT? HOW--?
TRUST ME. YOU DON'T WANT TO KNOW. LET'S JUST SAY WE HAVE TO KEEP FEEDING HIM BEANS, OR ELSE HE DOESN'T... GARNISH ANYMORE.
AND OVER HERE, YOU'LL FIND--
WAIT, WHAT'S IN THAT ROOM THERE? THE ONE THAT SAYS "CONTROL ROOM 4."
UH, ER, UM, YOU REALLY DON'T NEED TO SEE WHAT'S IN THAT ROOM.
UH, ER, UM, YES I DO. WHAT'S IN IT?
ER...WOULDN'T YOU RATHER SEE OUR BIG "CARDBOARDIUM EMPORIUM," WHERE WE MANUFACTURE ALL OF THE CARDBOARD FOR OUR CEREAL BOXES?
YOU SAY "ER" TOO MUCH FOR MY LIKING.
IT'S A LIFE-CHANGING EXPERIENCE, I ASSURE YOU!
MOVE AWAY FROM THE DOOR. NOW.

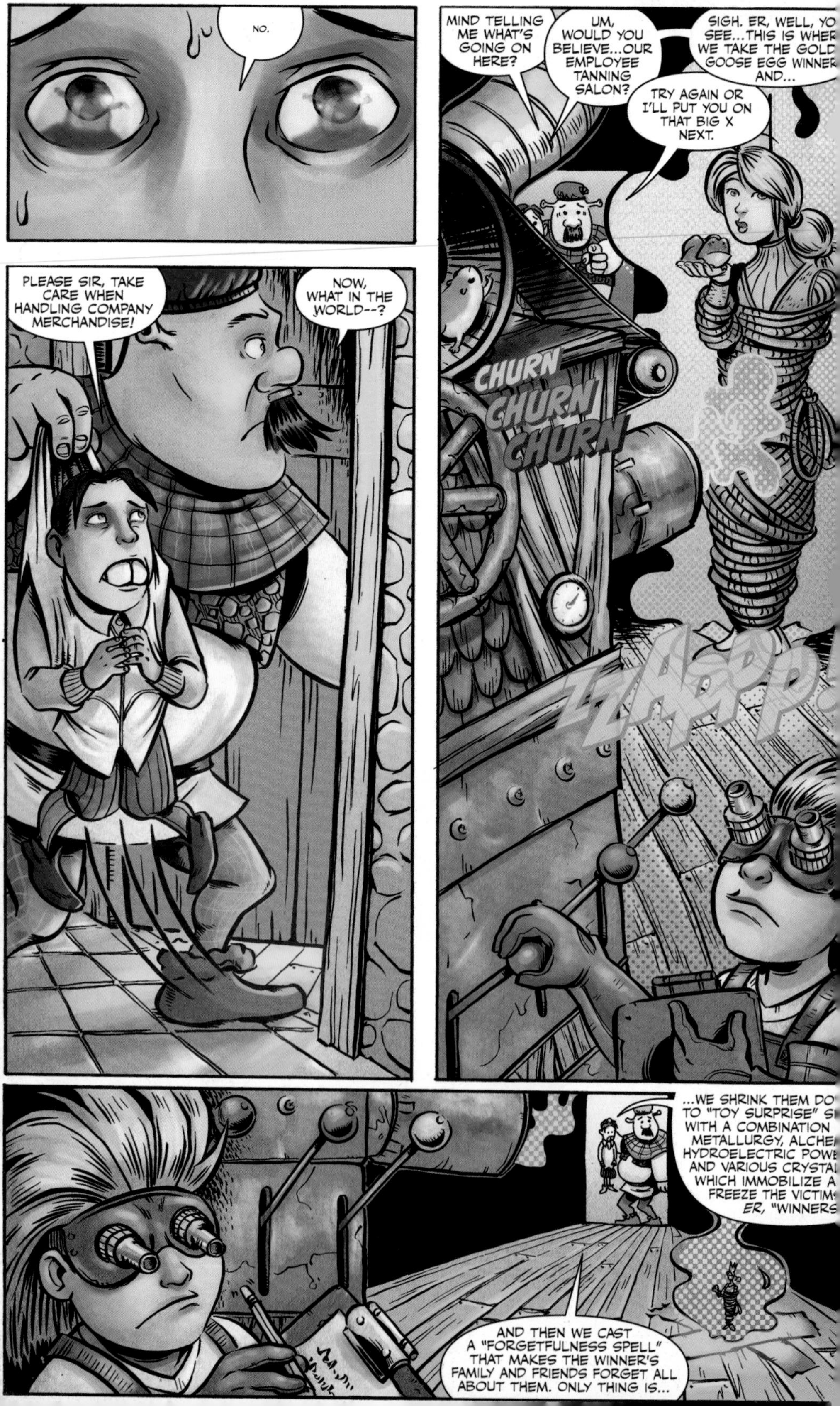
NO.
PLEASE SIR, TAKE CARE WHEN HANDLING COMPANY MERCHANDISE!
NOW, WHAT IN THE WORLD--?
MIND TELLING ME WHAT'S GOING ON HERE?
UM, WOULD YOU BELIEVE...OUR EMPLOYEE TANNING SALON?
SIGH. ER, WELL, YO SEE...THIS IS WHER WE TAKE THE GOLD GOOSE EGG WINNER AND...
TRY AGAIN OR I'LL PUT YOU ON THAT BIG X NEXT.
CHURN CHURN CHURN
ZZAPP!
...WE SHRINK THEM DO TO "TOY SURPRISE" S WITH A COMBINATION METALLURGY, ALCHE HYDROELECTRIC POWE AND VARIOUS CRYSTA WHICH IMMOBILIZE A FREEZE THE VICTIMS ER, "WINNERS
AND THEN WE CAST A "FORGETFULNESS SPELL" THAT MAKES THE WINNER'S FAMILY AND FRIENDS FORGET ALL ABOUT THEM. ONLY THING IS...

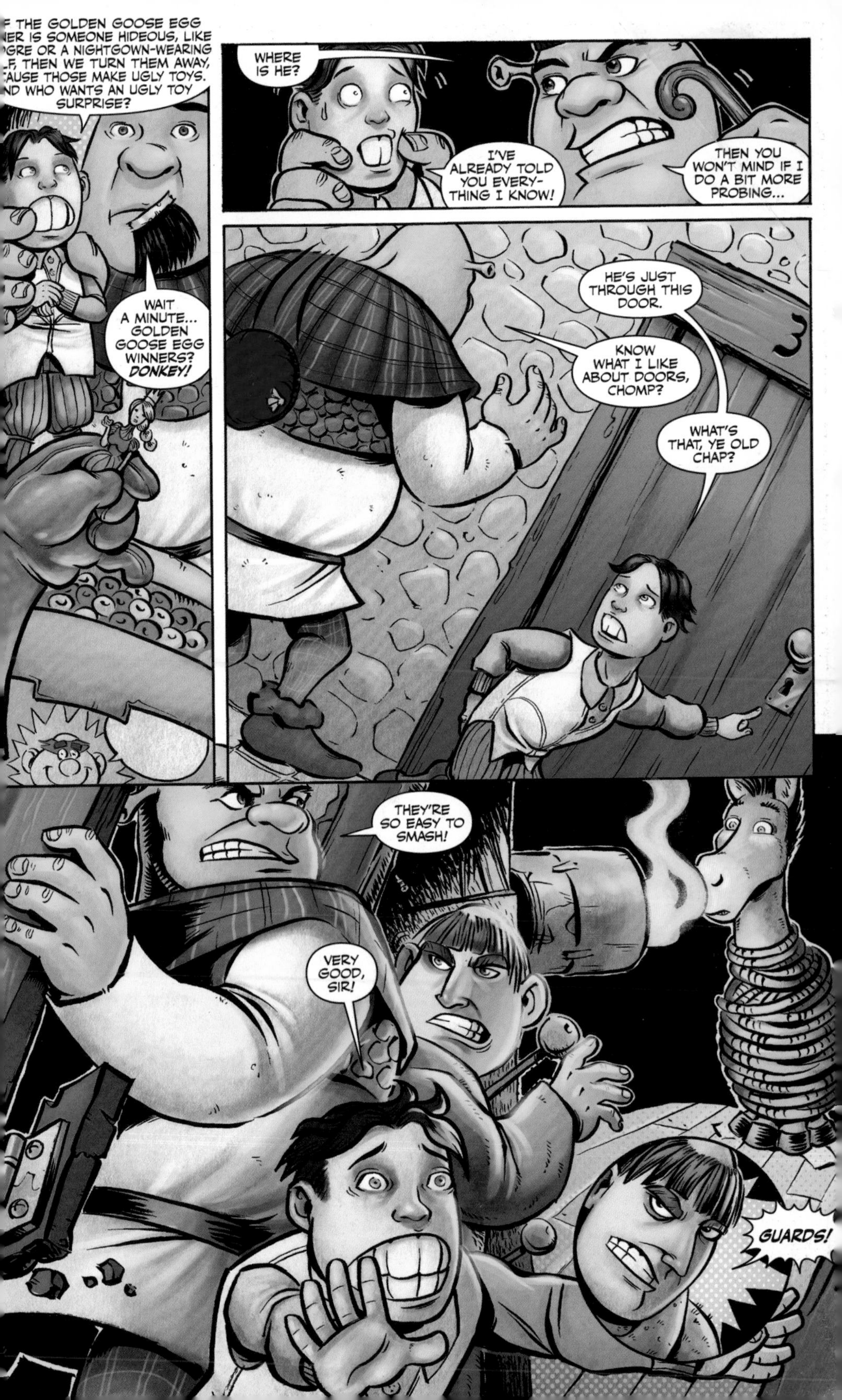
F THE GOLDEN GOOSE EGG NER IS SOMEONE HIDEOUS, LIKE OGRE OR A NIGHTGOWN-WEARING LF, THEN WE TURN THEM AWAY, CAUSE THOSE MAKE UGLY TOYS. ND WHO WANTS AN UGLY TOY SURPRISE?
WAIT A MINUTE... GOLDEN GOOSE EGG WINNERS? DONKEY!
WHERE IS HE?
I'VE ALREADY TOLD YOU EVERY-THING I KNOW!
THEN YOU WON'T MIND IF I DO A BIT MORE PROBING...
HE'S JUST THROUGH THIS DOOR.
KNOW WHAT I LIKE ABOUT DOORS, CHOMP?
WHAT'S THAT, YE OLD CHAP?
THEY'RE SO EASY TO SMASH!
VERY GOOD, SIR!
GUARDS!

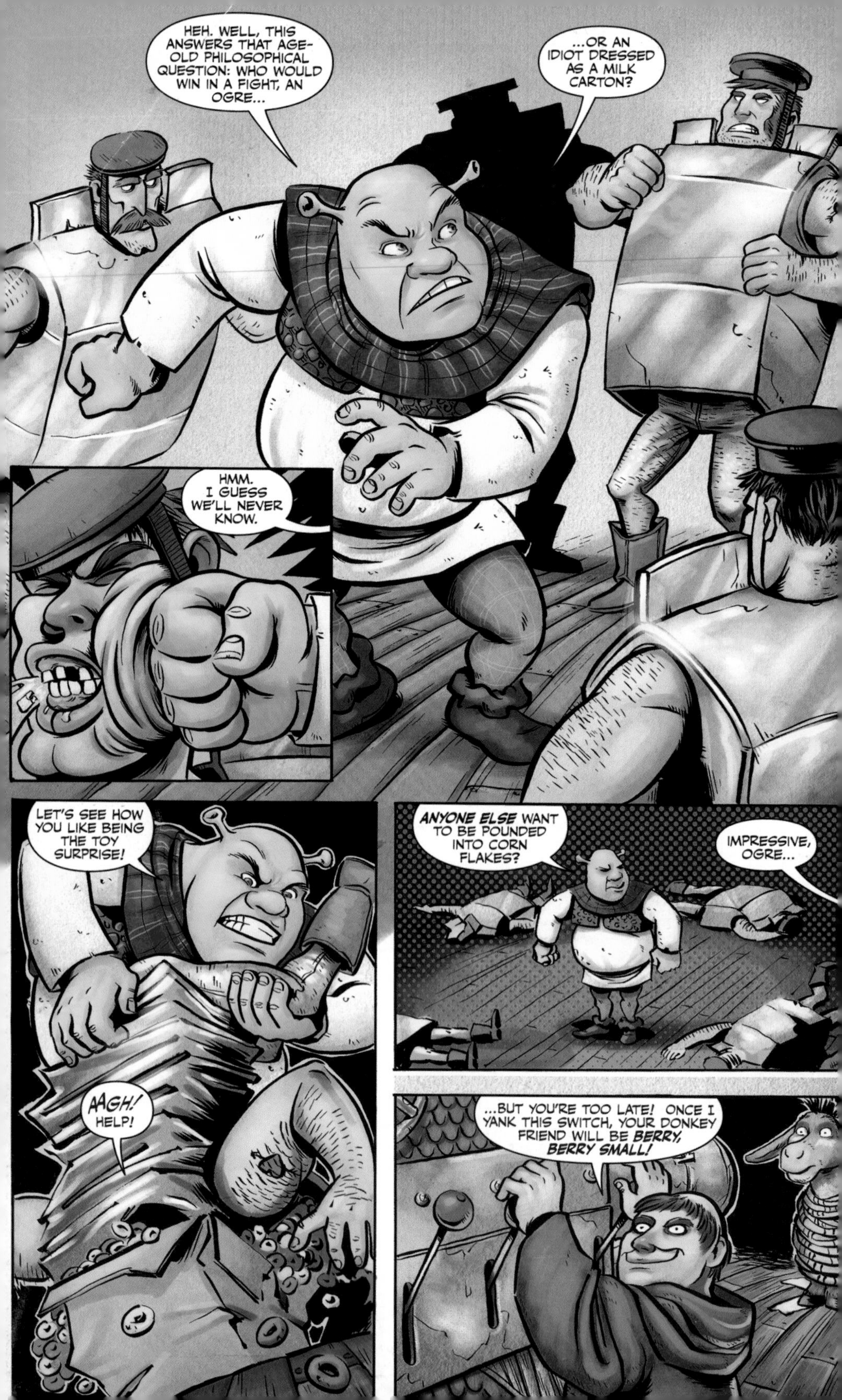
HEH. WELL, THIS ANSWERS THAT AGE-OLD PHILOSOPHICAL QUESTION: WHO WOULD WIN IN A FIGHT, AN OGRE...
...OR AN IDIOT DRESSED AS A MILK CARTON?
HMM. I GUESS WE'LL NEVER KNOW.
LET'S SEE HOW YOU LIKE BEING THE TOY SURPRISE!
AAGH! HELP!
ANYONE ELSE WANT TO BE POUNDED INTO CORN FLAKES?
IMPRESSIVE, OGRE...
...BUT YOU'RE TOO LATE! ONCE I YANK THIS SWITCH, YOUR DONKEY FRIEND WILL BE BERRY, BERRY SMALL!

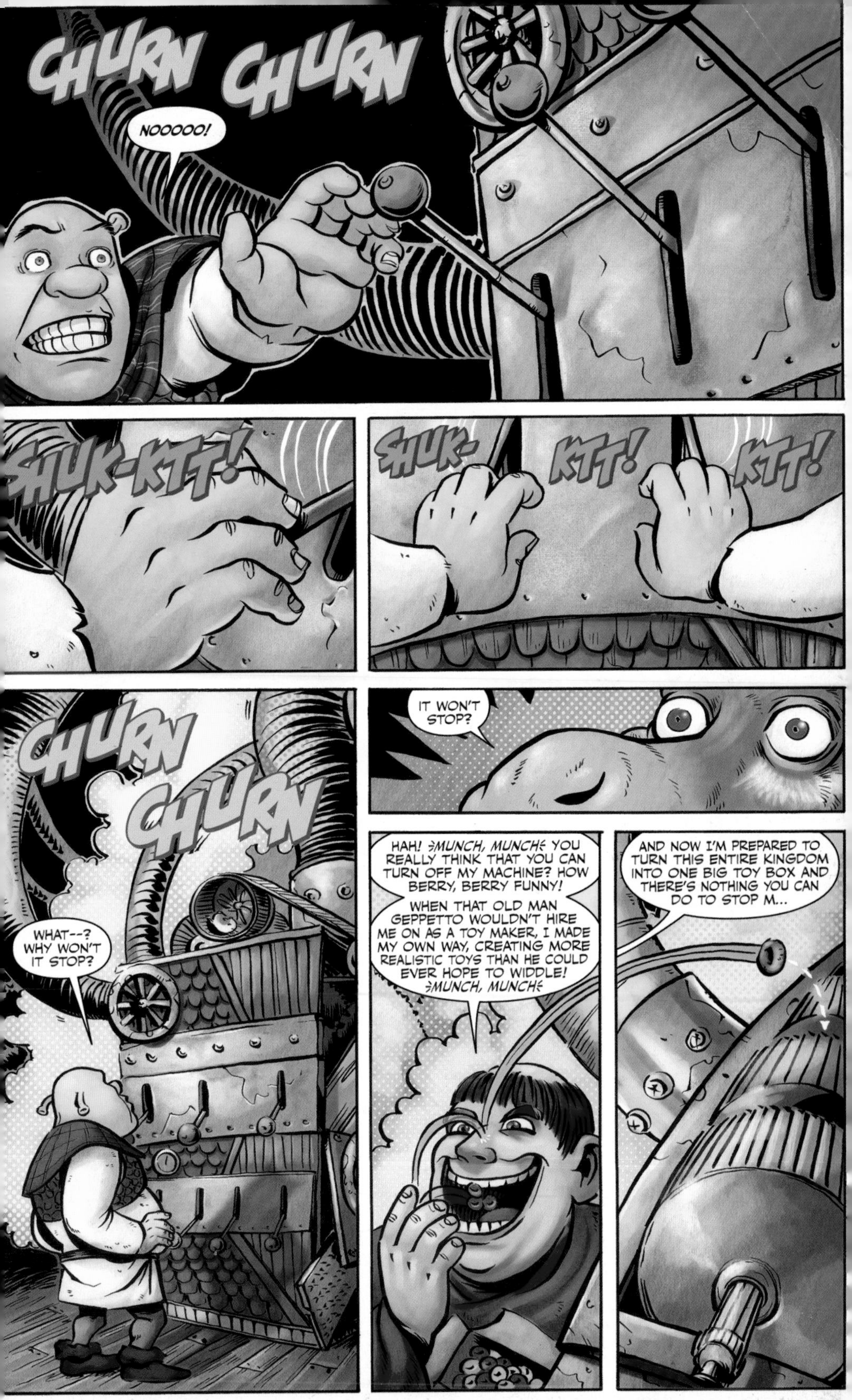
CHURN CHURN
NOOOOO!
SHUK-KTT!
SHUK-
KTT!
KTT!
CHURN
CHURN
WHAT--? WHY WON'T IT STOP?
IT WON'T STOP?
HAH! *MUNCH, MUNCH* YOU REALLY THINK THAT YOU CAN TURN OFF MY MACHINE? HOW BERRY, BERRY FUNNY!
WHEN THAT OLD MAN GEPPETTO WOULDN'T HIRE ME ON AS A TOY MAKER, I MADE MY OWN WAY, CREATING MORE REALISTIC TOYS THAN HE COULD EVER HOPE TO WIDDLE! *MUNCH, MUNCH*
AND NOW I'M PREPARED TO TURN THIS ENTIRE KINGDOM INTO ONE BIG TOY BOX AND THERE'S NOTHING YOU CAN DO TO STOP M...

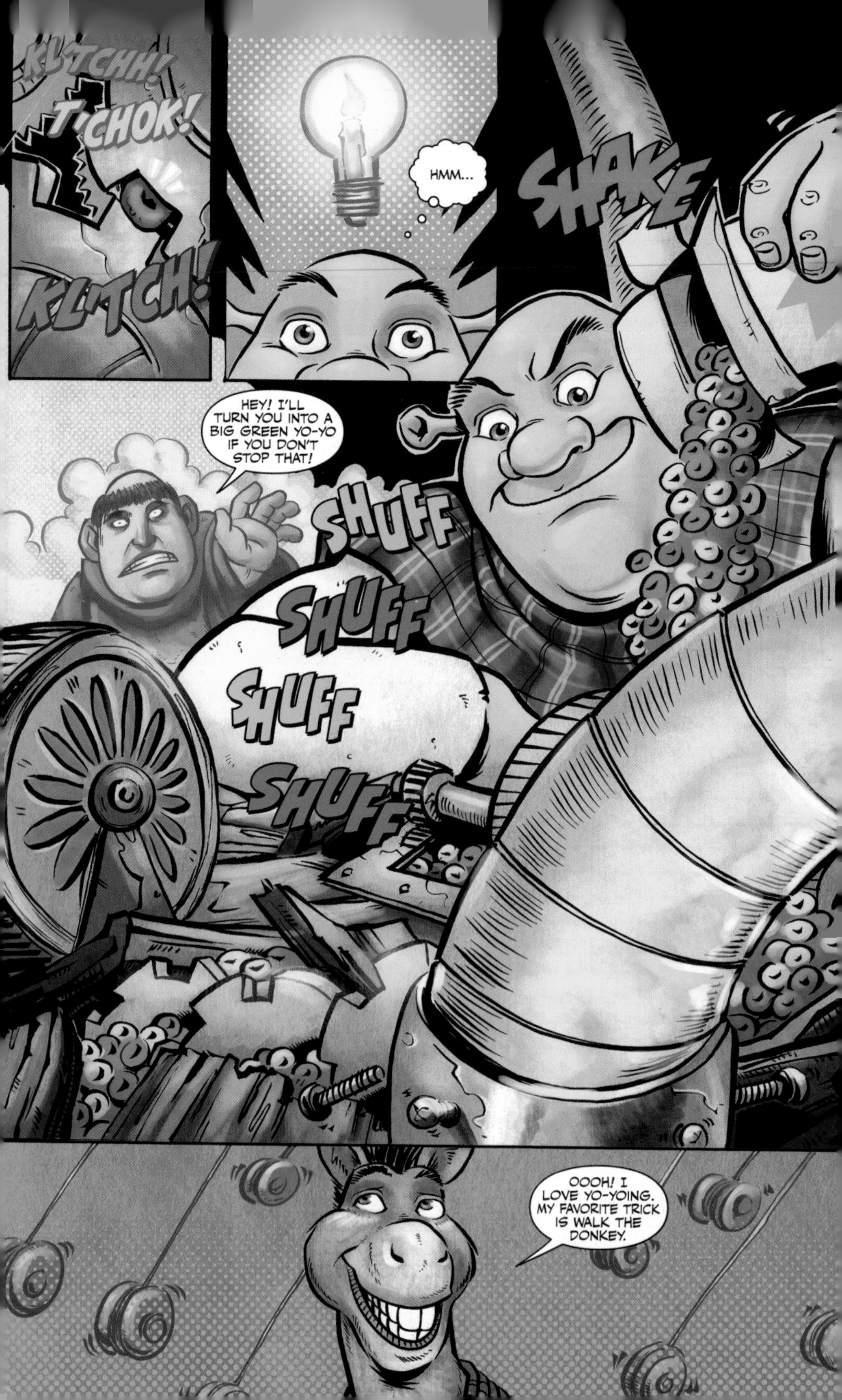
KL'TCHH!
T'CHOK!
KL'TCH!
HMM...
SHAKE
HEY! I'LL TURN YOU INTO A BIG GREEN YO-YO IF YOU DON'T STOP THAT!
SHUFF
SHUFF
SHUFF
SHUFF
OOOH! I LOVE YO-YOING. MY FAVORITE TRICK IS WALK THE DONKEY.

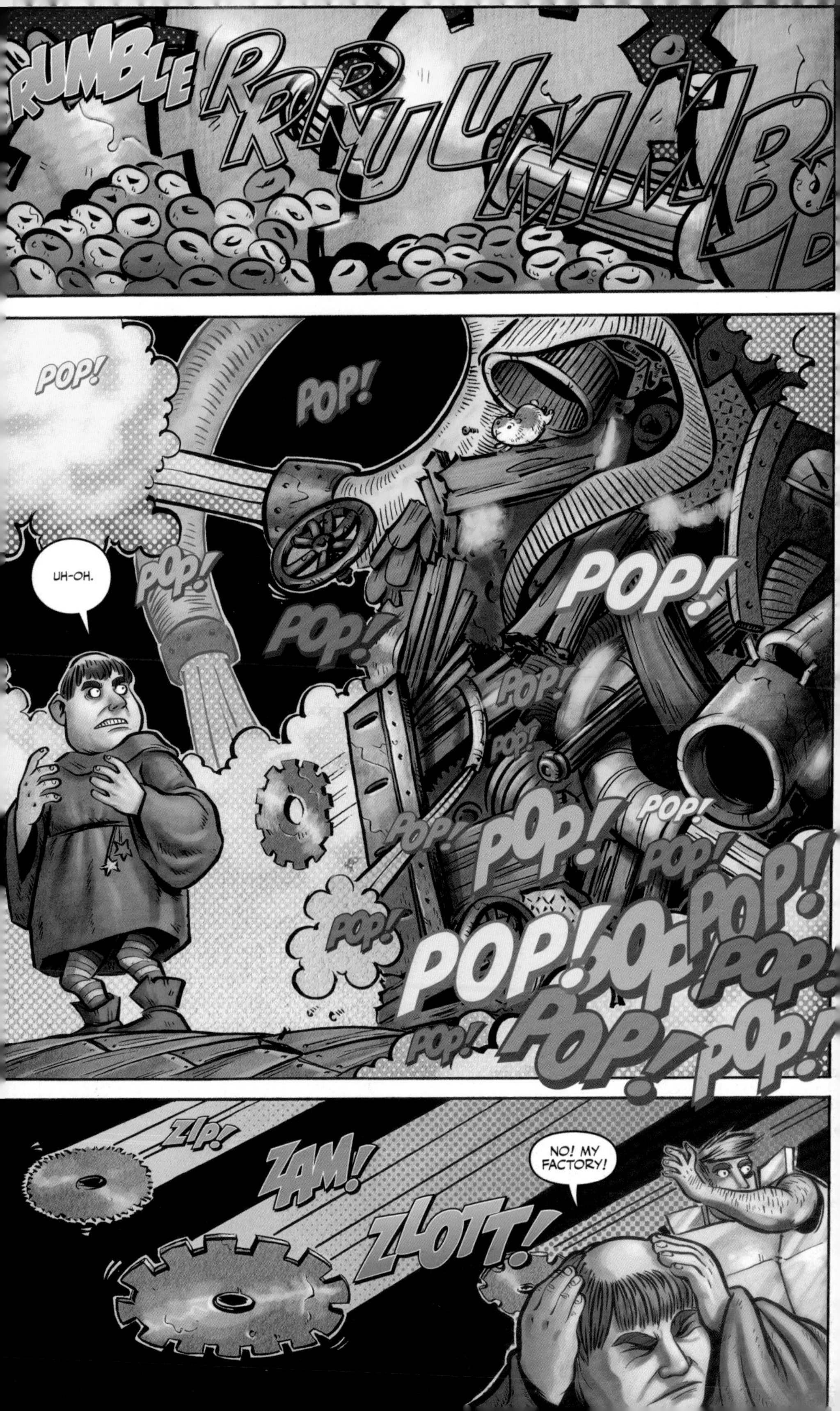
RUMBLE
RRRUUMMBB
POP!
POP!
UH-OH.
POP!
POP!
POP!
POP!
POP!
POP!
POP!
POP!
POP!
POP!
POP!
POP!
POP!
POP!
POP!
POP!
ZIP!
ZAM!
ZLOTT!
NO! MY FACTORY!

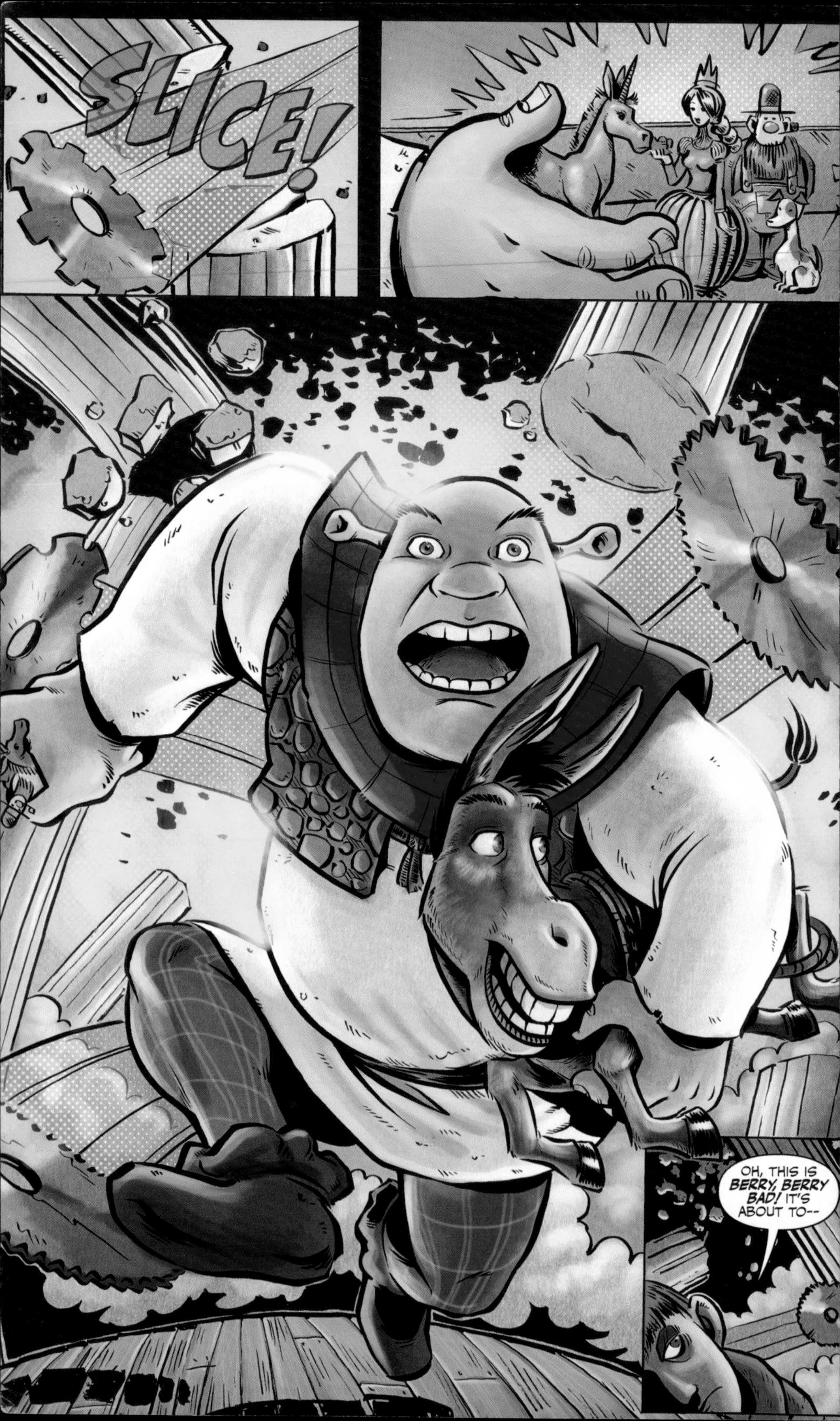
SLICE!
OH, THIS IS BERRY, BERRY BAD! IT'S ABOUT TO--

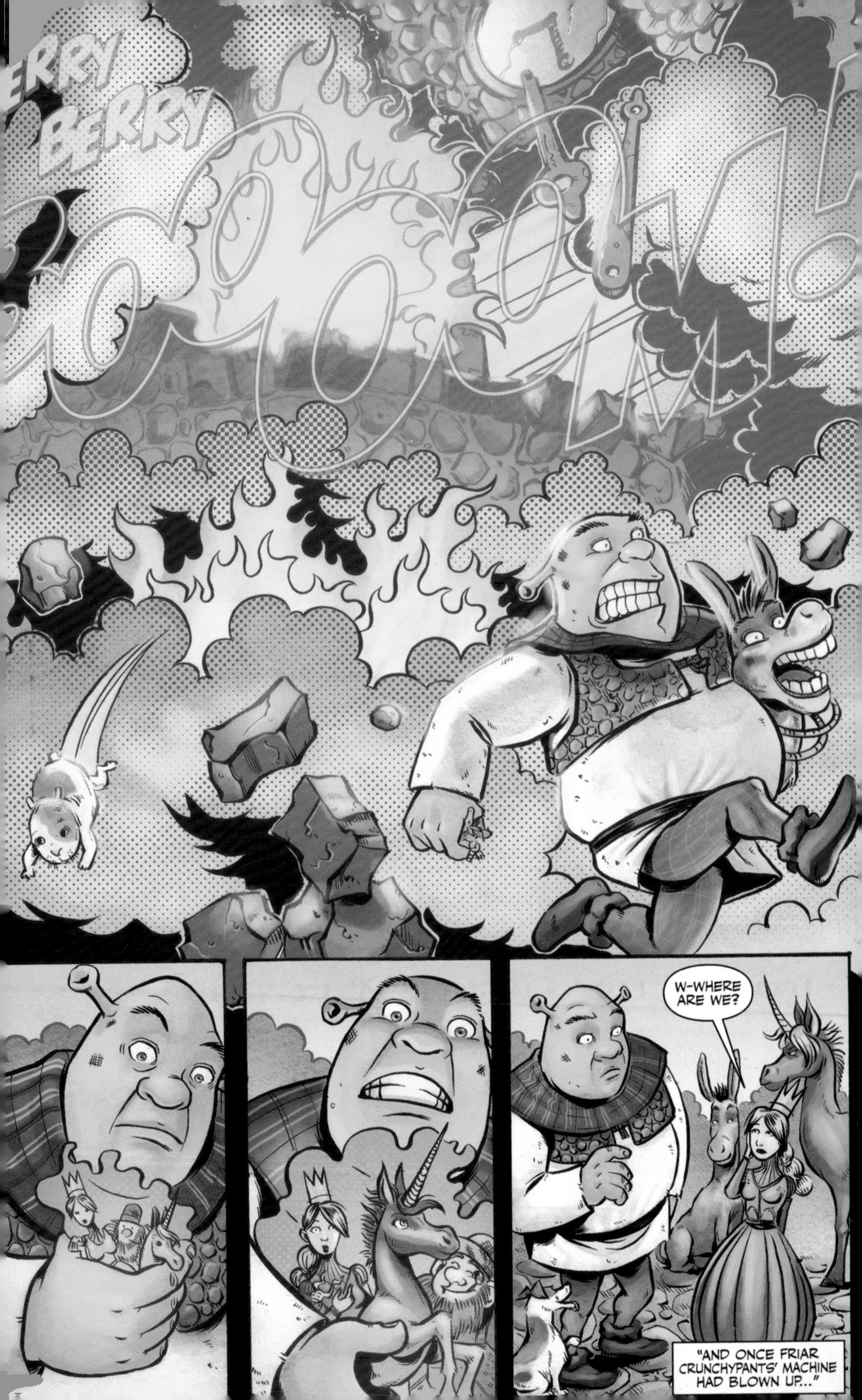

ERRY BERRY
BERRY
ZOOOOOOOOM!
W-WHERE ARE WE?
"AND ONCE FRIAR CRUNCHYPANTS' MACHINE HAD BLOWN UP..."

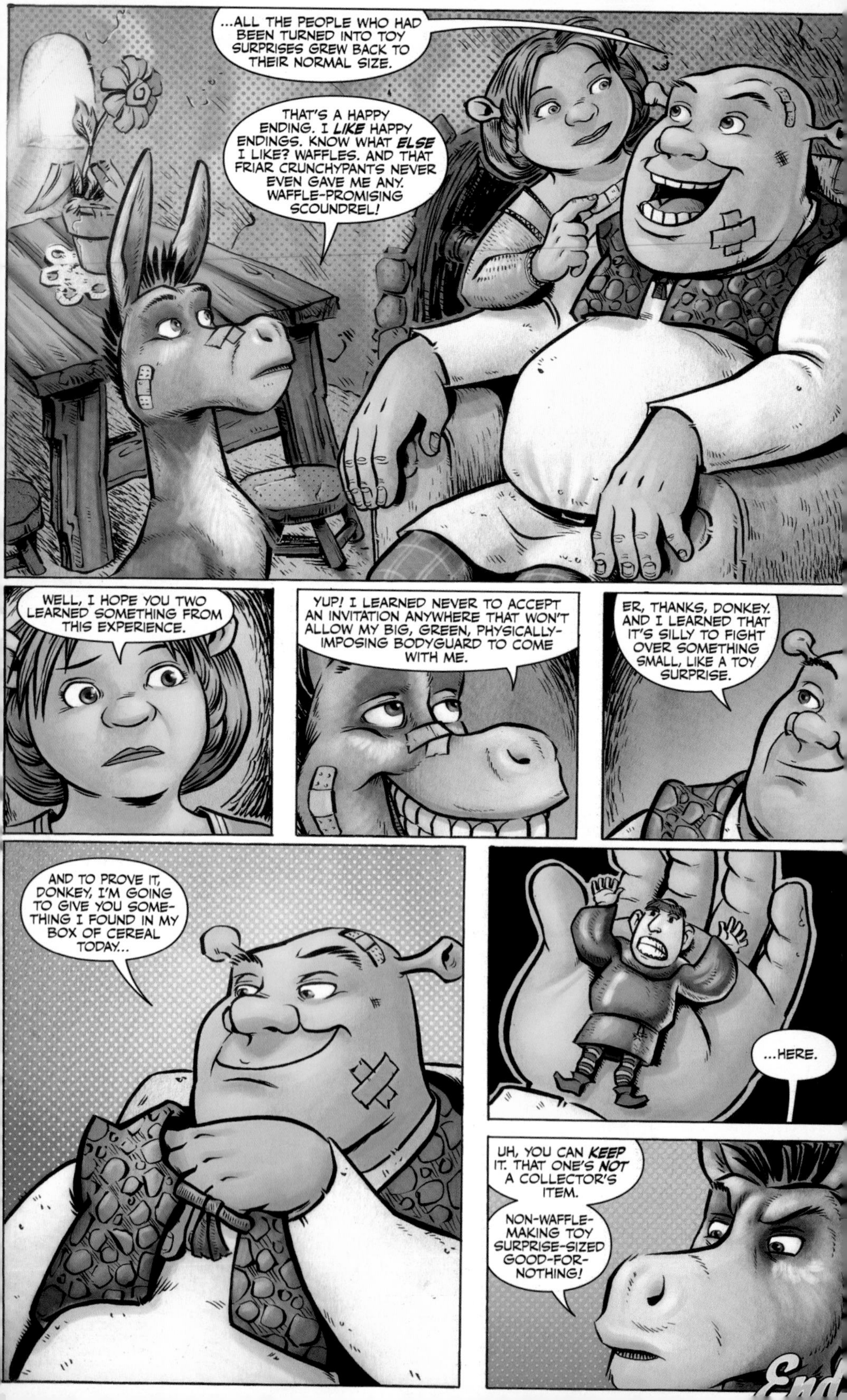
...ALL THE PEOPLE WHO HAD BEEN TURNED INTO TOY SURPRISES GREW BACK TO THEIR NORMAL SIZE.
THAT'S A HAPPY ENDING. I *LIKE* HAPPY ENDINGS. KNOW WHAT *ELSE* I LIKE? WAFFLES. AND THAT FRIAR CRUNCHYPANTS NEVER EVEN GAVE ME ANY. WAFFLE-PROMISING SCOUNDREL!
WELL, I HOPE YOU TWO LEARNED SOMETHING FROM THIS EXPERIENCE.
YUP! I LEARNED NEVER TO ACCEPT AN INVITATION ANYWHERE THAT WON'T ALLOW MY BIG, GREEN, PHYSICALLY-IMPOSING BODYGUARD TO COME WITH ME.
ER, THANKS, DONKEY. AND I LEARNED THAT IT'S SILLY TO FIGHT OVER SOMETHING SMALL, LIKE A TOY SURPRISE.
AND TO PROVE IT, DONKEY, I'M GOING TO GIVE YOU SOME-THING I FOUND IN MY BOX OF CEREAL TODAY...
...HERE.
UH, YOU CAN *KEEP* IT. THAT ONE'S *NOT* A COLLECTOR'S ITEM.
NON-WAFFLE-MAKING TOY SURPRISE-SIZED GOOD-FOR-NOTHING!
End

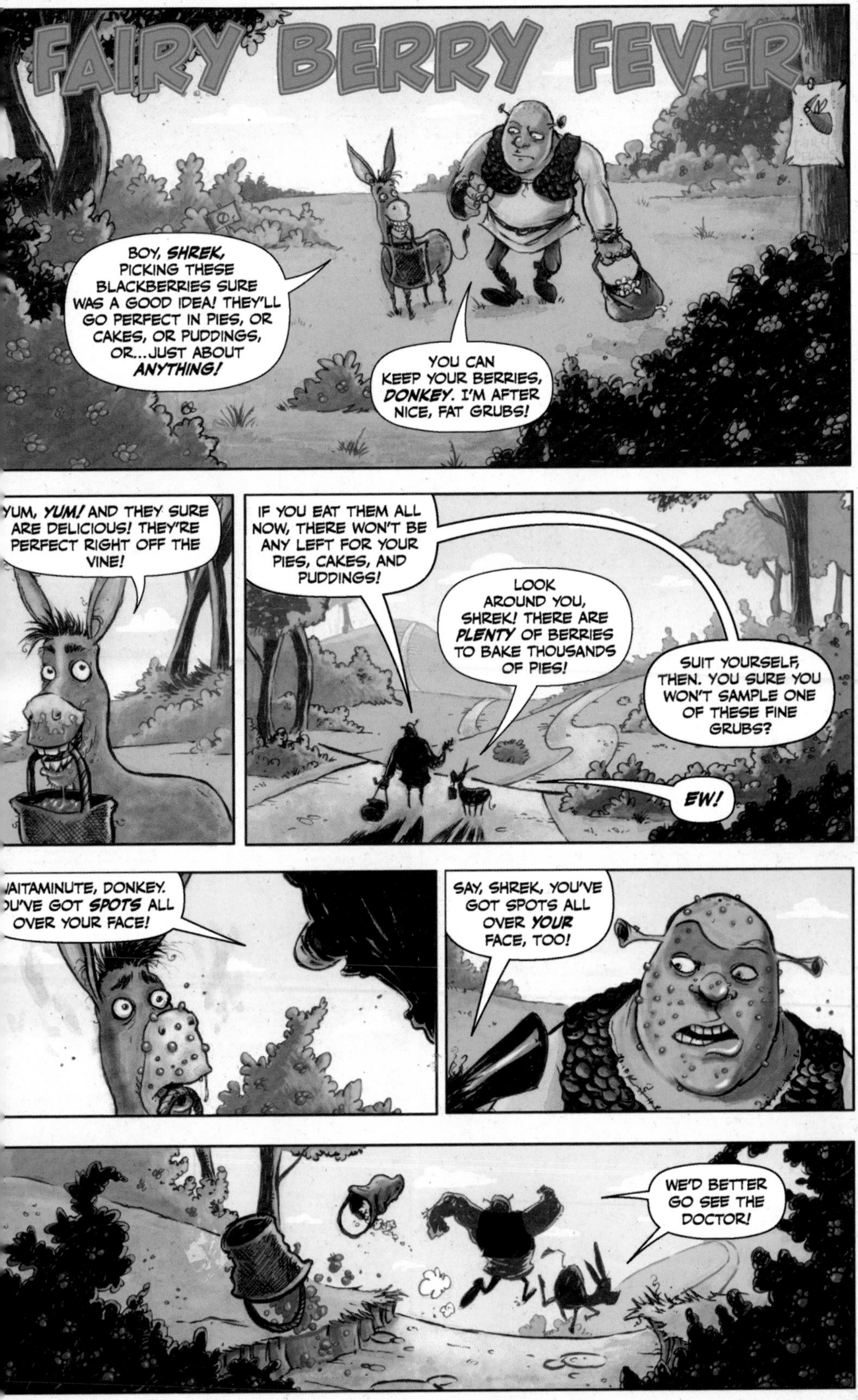
FAIRY BERRY FEVER
BOY, SHREK, PICKING THESE BLACKBERRIES SURE WAS A GOOD IDEA! THEY'LL GO PERFECT IN PIES, OR CAKES, OR PUDDINGS, OR...JUST ABOUT ANYTHING!
YOU CAN KEEP YOUR BERRIES, DONKEY. I'M AFTER NICE, FAT GRUBS!
YUM, YUM! AND THEY SURE ARE DELICIOUS! THEY'RE PERFECT RIGHT OFF THE VINE!
IF YOU EAT THEM ALL NOW, THERE WON'T BE ANY LEFT FOR YOUR PIES, CAKES, AND PUDDINGS!
LOOK AROUND YOU, SHREK! THERE ARE PLENTY OF BERRIES TO BAKE THOUSANDS OF PIES!
SUIT YOURSELF, THEN. YOU SURE YOU WON'T SAMPLE ONE OF THESE FINE GRUBS?
EW!
AITAMINUTE, DONKEY. OU'VE GOT SPOTS ALL OVER YOUR FACE!
SAY, SHREK, YOU'VE GOT SPOTS ALL OVER YOUR FACE, TOO!
WE'D BETTER GO SEE THE DOCTOR!

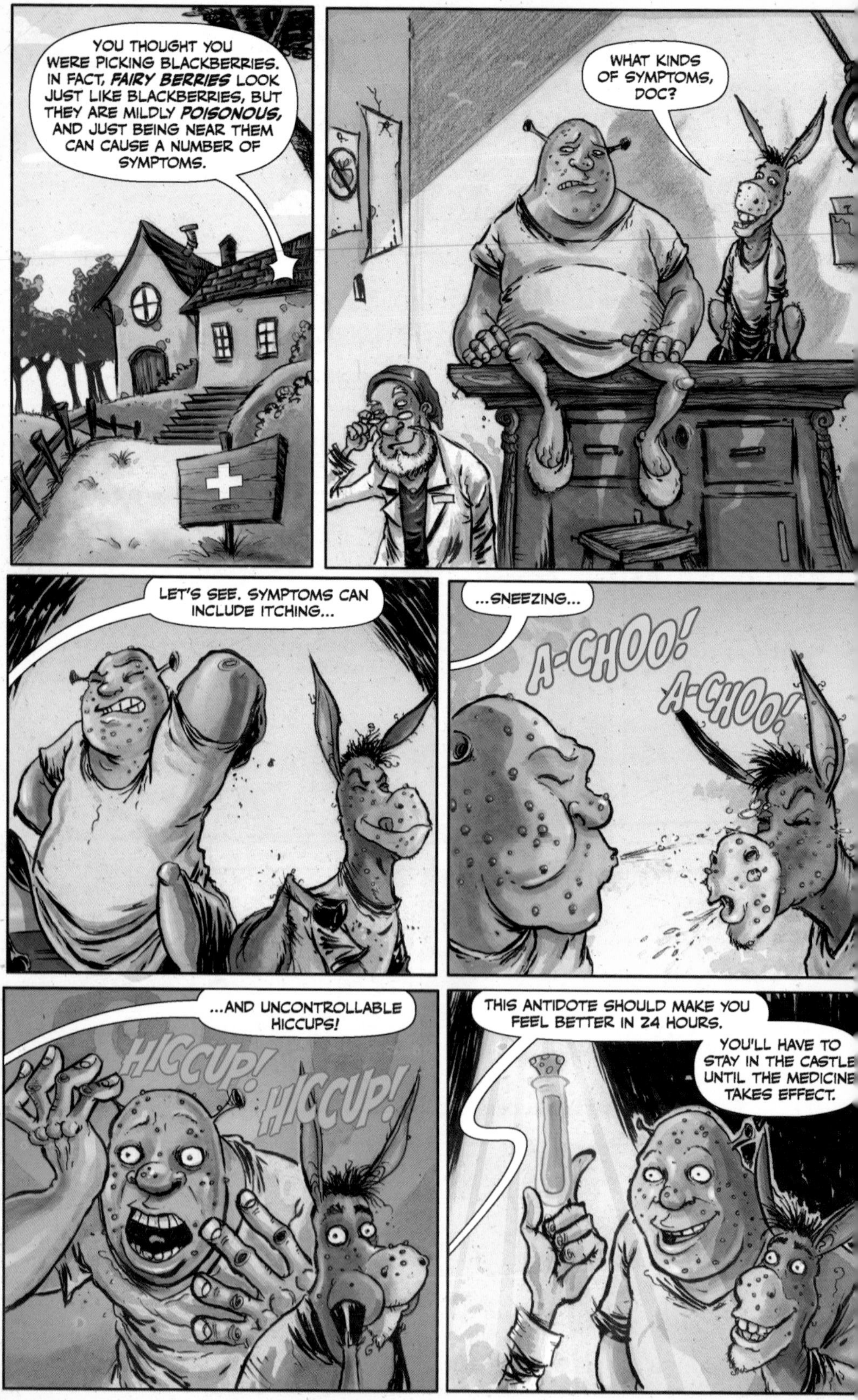
YOU THOUGHT YOU WERE PICKING BLACKBERRIES. IN FACT, *FAIRY BERRIES* LOOK JUST LIKE BLACKBERRIES, BUT THEY ARE MILDLY *POISONOUS,* AND JUST BEING NEAR THEM CAN CAUSE A NUMBER OF SYMPTOMS.
WHAT KINDS OF SYMPTOMS, DOC?
LET'S SEE. SYMPTOMS CAN INCLUDE ITCHING...
...SNEEZING...
A-CHOO!
A-CHOO!
...AND UNCONTROLLABLE HICCUPS!
HICCUP!
HICCUP!
THIS ANTIDOTE SHOULD MAKE YOU FEEL BETTER IN 24 HOURS.
YOU'LL HAVE TO STAY IN THE CASTLE UNTIL THE MEDICINE TAKES EFFECT.

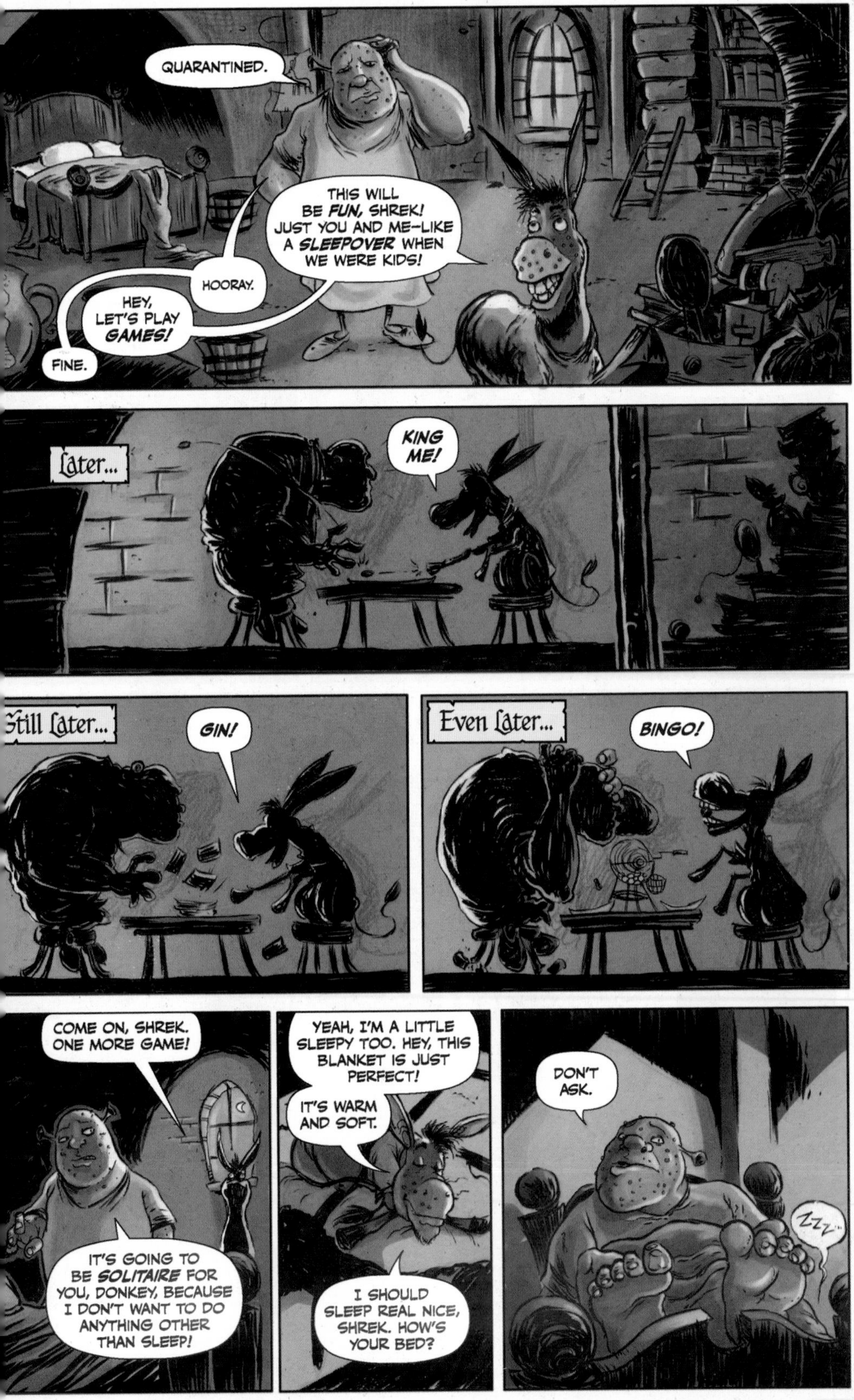
QUARANTINED.
THIS WILL BE FUN, SHREK! JUST YOU AND ME—LIKE A SLEEPOVER WHEN WE WERE KIDS!
HOORAY.
HEY, LET'S PLAY GAMES!
FINE.
Later...
KING ME!
Still Later...
GIN!
Even Later...
BINGO!
COME ON, SHREK. ONE MORE GAME!
IT'S GOING TO BE SOLITAIRE FOR YOU, DONKEY, BECAUSE I DON'T WANT TO DO ANYTHING OTHER THAN SLEEP!
YEAH, I'M A LITTLE SLEEPY TOO. HEY, THIS BLANKET IS JUST PERFECT!
IT'S WARM AND SOFT.
I SHOULD SLEEP REAL NICE, SHREK. HOW'S YOUR BED?
DON'T ASK.
ZZZ...

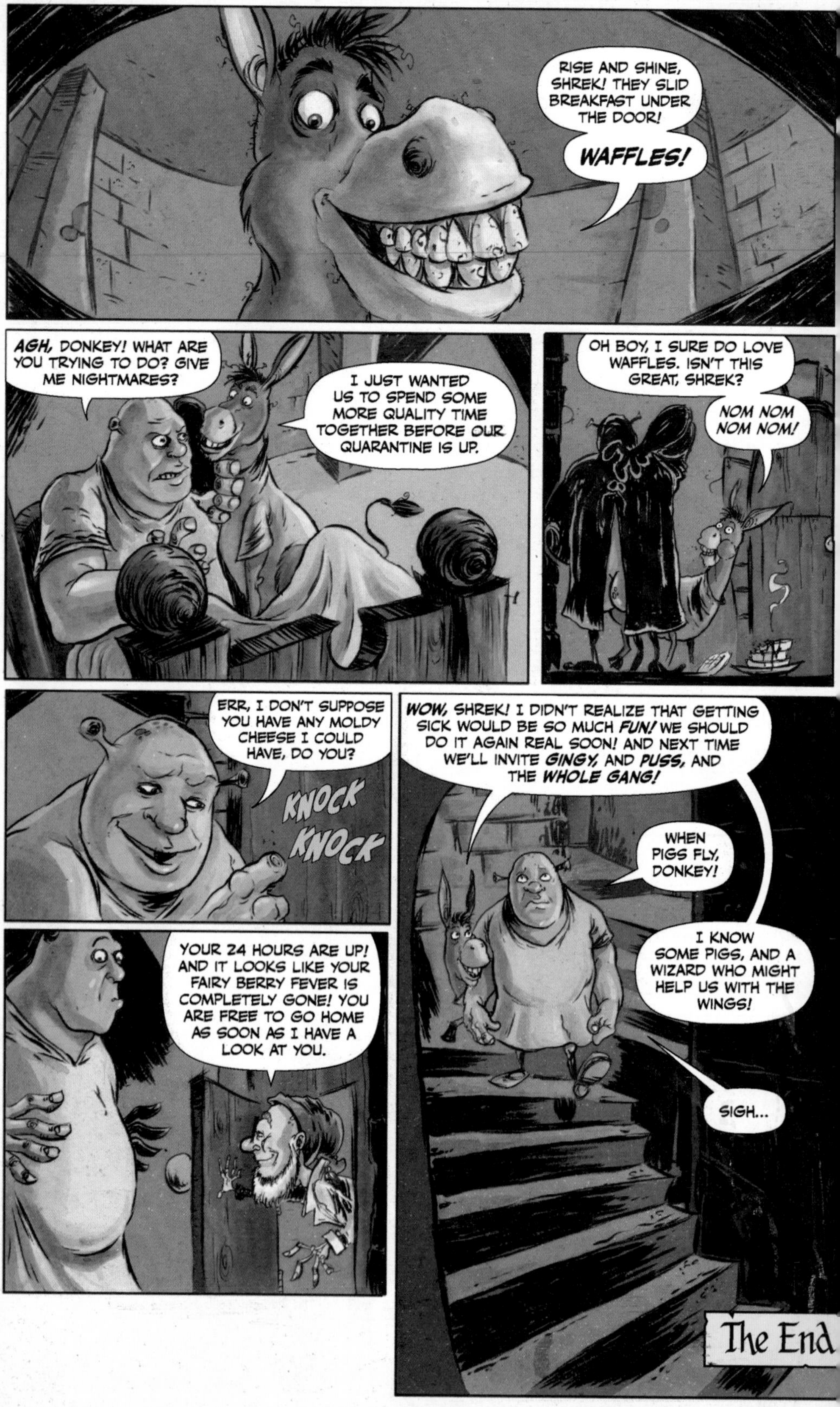

RISE AND SHINE, SHREK! THEY SLID BREAKFAST UNDER THE DOOR!
WAFFLES!
AGH, DONKEY! WHAT ARE YOU TRYING TO DO? GIVE ME NIGHTMARES?
I JUST WANTED US TO SPEND SOME MORE QUALITY TIME TOGETHER BEFORE OUR QUARANTINE IS UP.
OH BOY, I SURE DO LOVE WAFFLES. ISN'T THIS GREAT, SHREK?
NOM NOM NOM NOM!
ERR, I DON'T SUPPOSE YOU HAVE ANY MOLDY CHEESE I COULD HAVE, DO YOU?
KNOCK
KNOCK
YOUR 24 HOURS ARE UP! AND IT LOOKS LIKE YOUR FAIRY BERRY FEVER IS COMPLETELY GONE! YOU ARE FREE TO GO HOME AS SOON AS I HAVE A LOOK AT YOU.
WOW, SHREK! I DIDN'T REALIZE THAT GETTING SICK WOULD BE SO MUCH FUN! WE SHOULD DO IT AGAIN REAL SOON! AND NEXT TIME WE'LL INVITE GINGY, AND PUSS, AND THE WHOLE GANG!
WHEN PIGS FLY, DONKEY!
I KNOW SOME PIGS, AND A WIZARD WHO MIGHT HELP US WITH THE WINGS!
SIGH...
The End

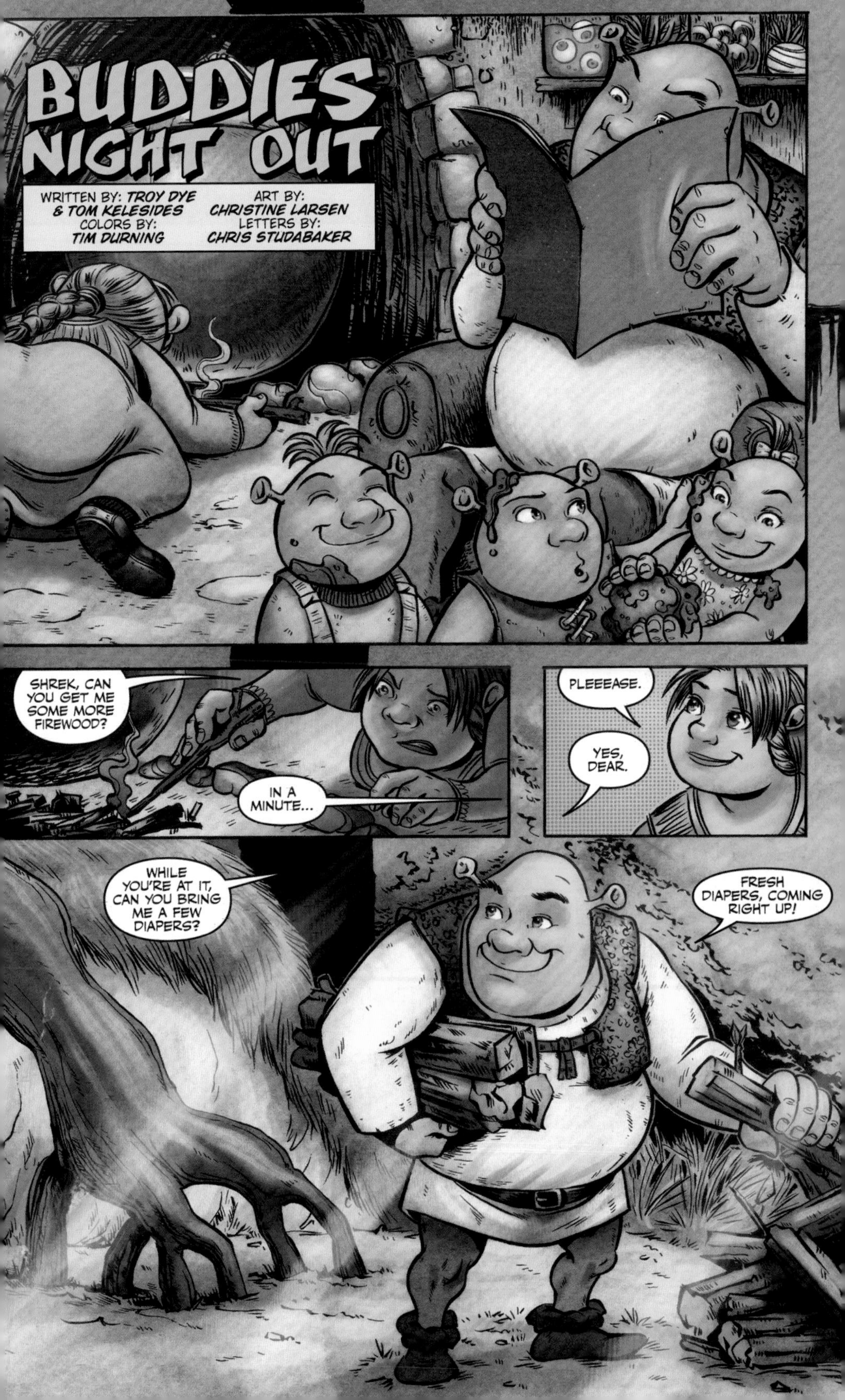
BUDDIES NIGHT OUT
WRITTEN BY: TROY DYE & TOM KELESIDES
ART BY: CHRISTINE LARSEN
COLORS BY: TIM DURNING
LETTERS BY: CHRIS STUDABAKER
SHREK, CAN YOU GET ME SOME MORE FIREWOOD?
IN A MINUTE...
PLEEEASE.
YES, DEAR.
WHILE YOU'RE AT IT, CAN YOU BRING ME A FEW DIAPERS?
FRESH DIAPERS, COMING RIGHT UP!

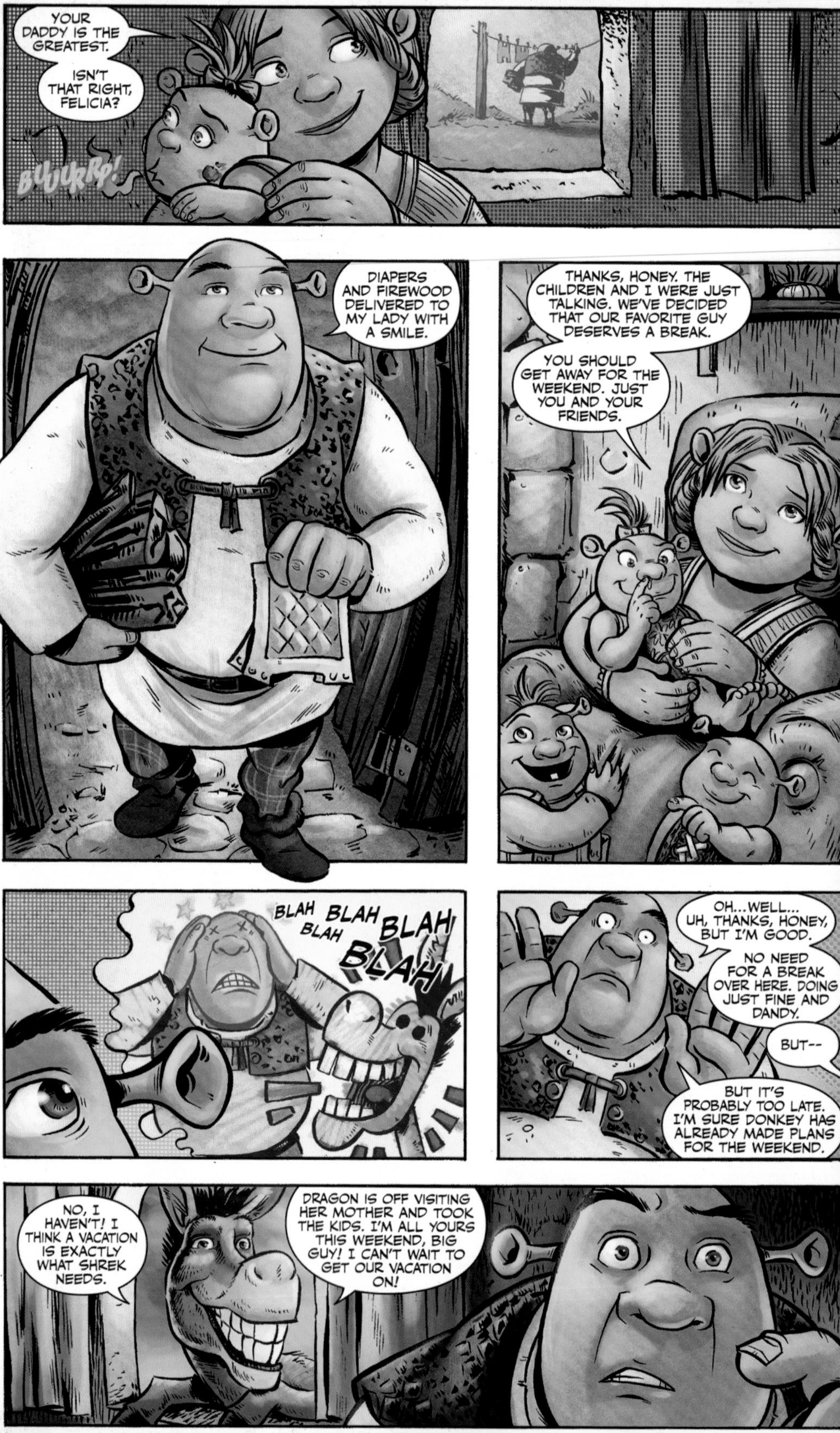
YOUR DADDY IS THE GREATEST.
ISN'T THAT RIGHT, FELICIA?
BLUURRP!
DIAPERS AND FIREWOOD DELIVERED TO MY LADY WITH A SMILE.
THANKS, HONEY. THE CHILDREN AND I WERE JUST TALKING. WE'VE DECIDED THAT OUR FAVORITE GUY DESERVES A BREAK.
YOU SHOULD GET AWAY FOR THE WEEKEND. JUST YOU AND YOUR FRIENDS.
BLAH BLAH BLAH BLAH BLAH
OH...WELL... UH, THANKS, HONEY, BUT I'M GOOD.
NO NEED FOR A BREAK OVER HERE. DOING JUST FINE AND DANDY.
BUT--
BUT IT'S PROBABLY TOO LATE. I'M SURE DONKEY HAS ALREADY MADE PLANS FOR THE WEEKEND.
NO, I HAVEN'T! I THINK A VACATION IS EXACTLY WHAT SHREK NEEDS.
DRAGON IS OFF VISITING HER MOTHER AND TOOK THE KIDS. I'M ALL YOURS THIS WEEKEND, BIG GUY! I CAN'T WAIT TO GET OUR VACATION ON!

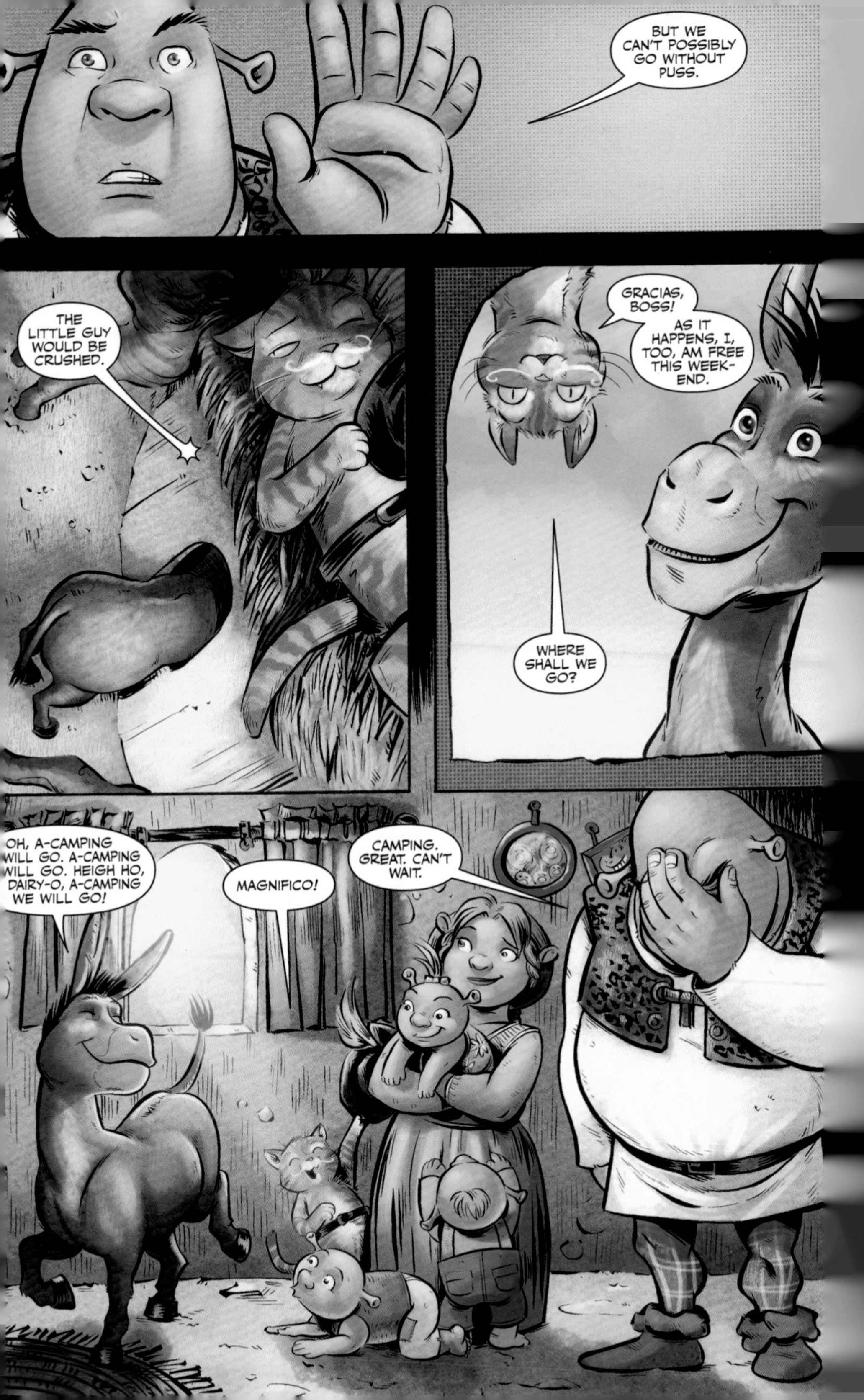
BUT WE CAN'T POSSIBLY GO WITHOUT PUSS.
THE LITTLE GUY WOULD BE CRUSHED.
GRACIAS, BOSS!
AS IT HAPPENS, I, TOO, AM FREE THIS WEEK-END.
WHERE SHALL WE GO?
OH, A-CAMPING WILL GO. A-CAMPING WILL GO. HEIGH HO, DAIRY-O, A-CAMPING WE WILL GO!
MAGNIFICO!
CAMPING. GREAT. CAN'T WAIT.

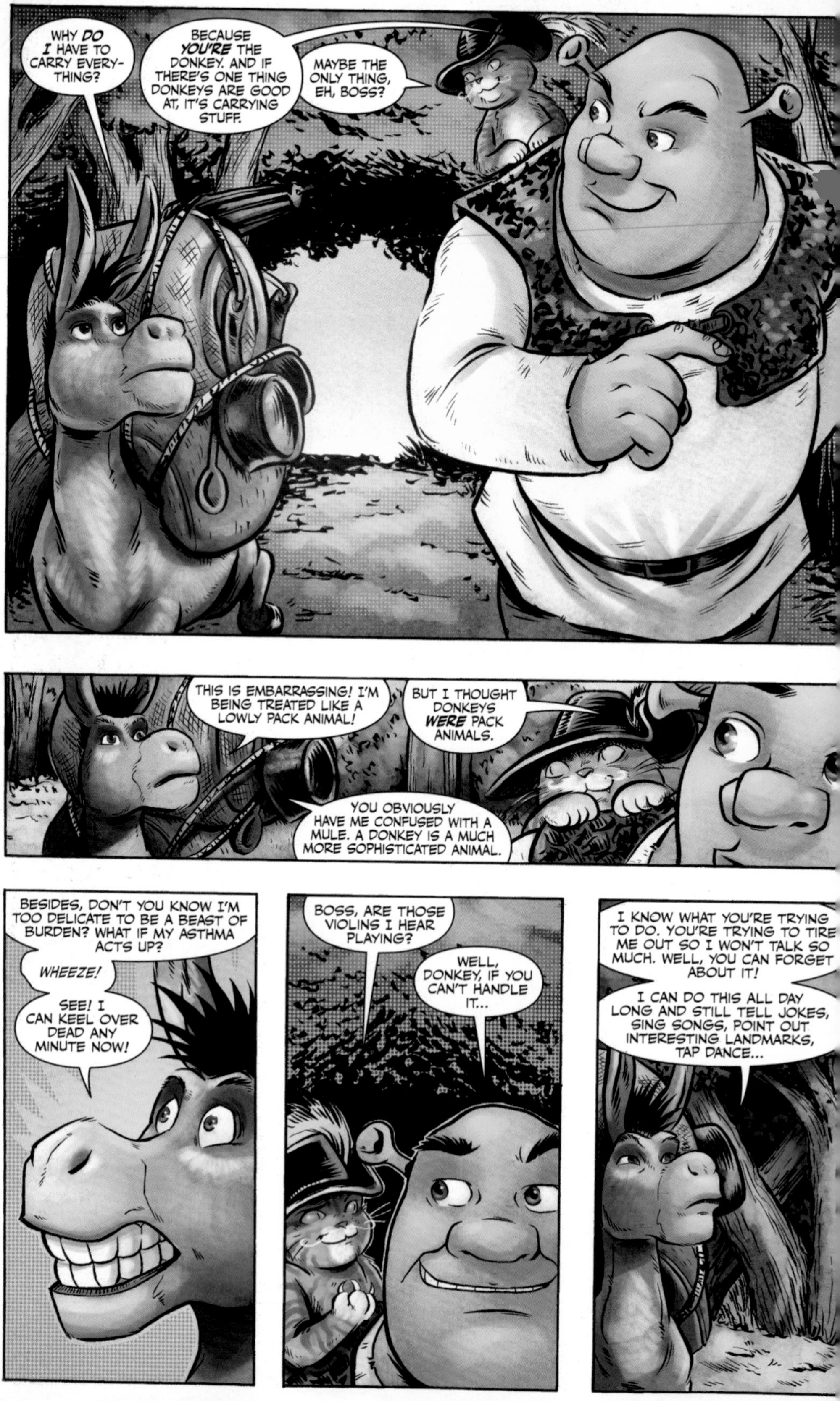
WHY DO I HAVE TO CARRY EVERY-THING?
BECAUSE YOU'RE THE DONKEY. AND IF THERE'S ONE THING DONKEYS ARE GOOD AT, IT'S CARRYING STUFF.
MAYBE THE ONLY THING, EH, BOSS?
THIS IS EMBARRASSING! I'M BEING TREATED LIKE A LOWLY PACK ANIMAL!
BUT I THOUGHT DONKEYS WERE PACK ANIMALS.
YOU OBVIOUSLY HAVE ME CONFUSED WITH A MULE. A DONKEY IS A MUCH MORE SOPHISTICATED ANIMAL.
BESIDES, DON'T YOU KNOW I'M TOO DELICATE TO BE A BEAST OF BURDEN? WHAT IF MY ASTHMA ACTS UP?
WHEEZE!
SEE! I CAN KEEL OVER DEAD ANY MINUTE NOW!
BOSS, ARE THOSE VIOLINS I HEAR PLAYING?
WELL, DONKEY, IF YOU CAN'T HANDLE IT...
I KNOW WHAT YOU'RE TRYING TO DO. YOU'RE TRYING TO TIRE ME OUT SO I WON'T TALK SO MUCH. WELL, YOU CAN FORGET ABOUT IT!
I CAN DO THIS ALL DAY LONG AND STILL TELL JOKES, SING SONGS, POINT OUT INTERESTING LANDMARKS, TAP DANCE...

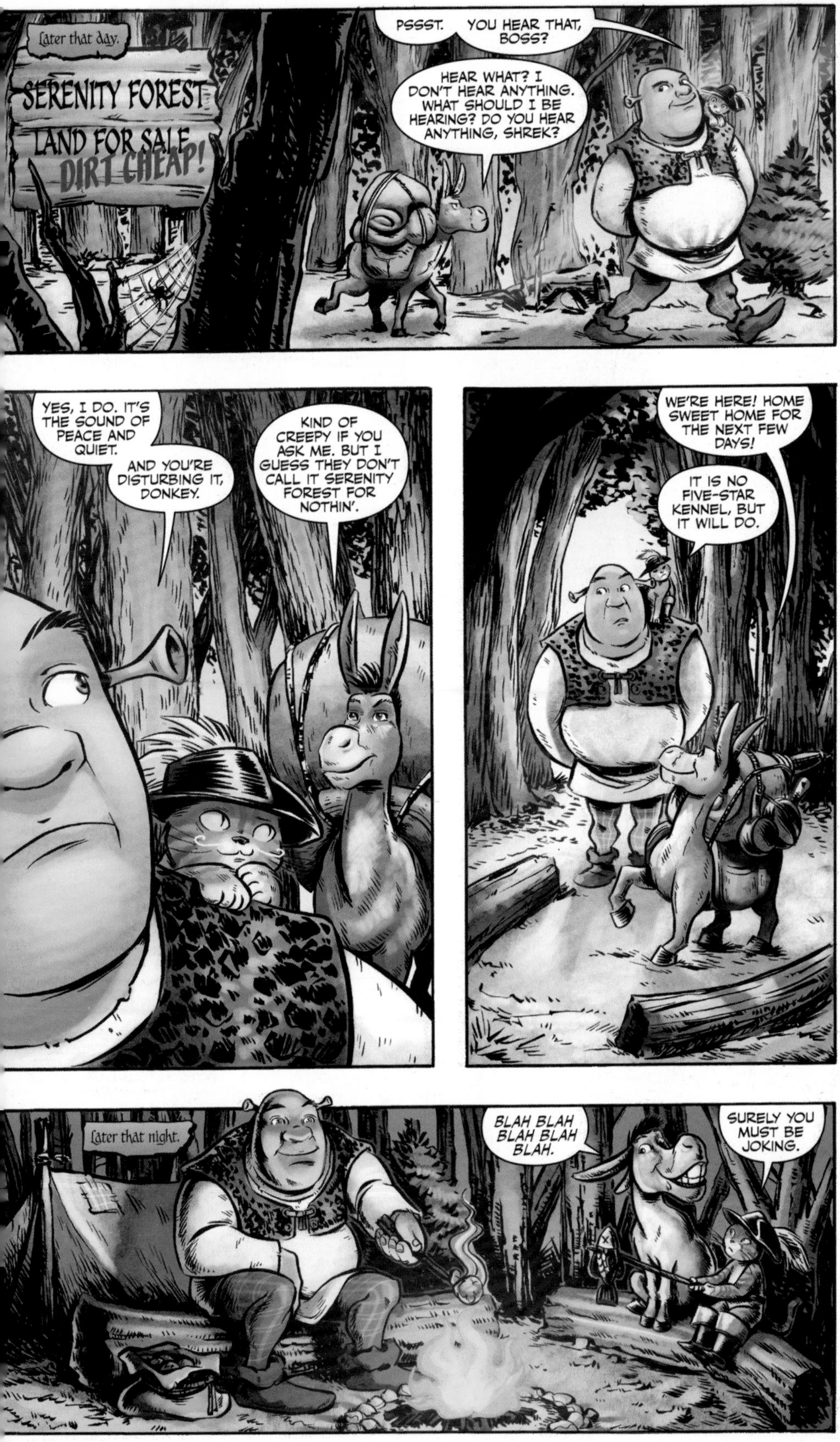
Later that day.
SERENITY FOREST
LAND FOR SALE
DIRT CHEAP!
PSSST.
YOU HEAR THAT, BOSS?
HEAR WHAT? I DON'T HEAR ANYTHING. WHAT SHOULD I BE HEARING? DO YOU HEAR ANYTHING, SHREK?
YES, I DO. IT'S THE SOUND OF PEACE AND QUIET.
AND YOU'RE DISTURBING IT, DONKEY.
KIND OF CREEPY IF YOU ASK ME. BUT I GUESS THEY DON'T CALL IT SERENITY FOREST FOR NOTHIN'.
WE'RE HERE! HOME SWEET HOME FOR THE NEXT FEW DAYS!
IT IS NO FIVE-STAR KENNEL, BUT IT WILL DO.
Later that night.
BLAH BLAH BLAH BLAH BLAH.
SURELY YOU MUST BE JOKING.

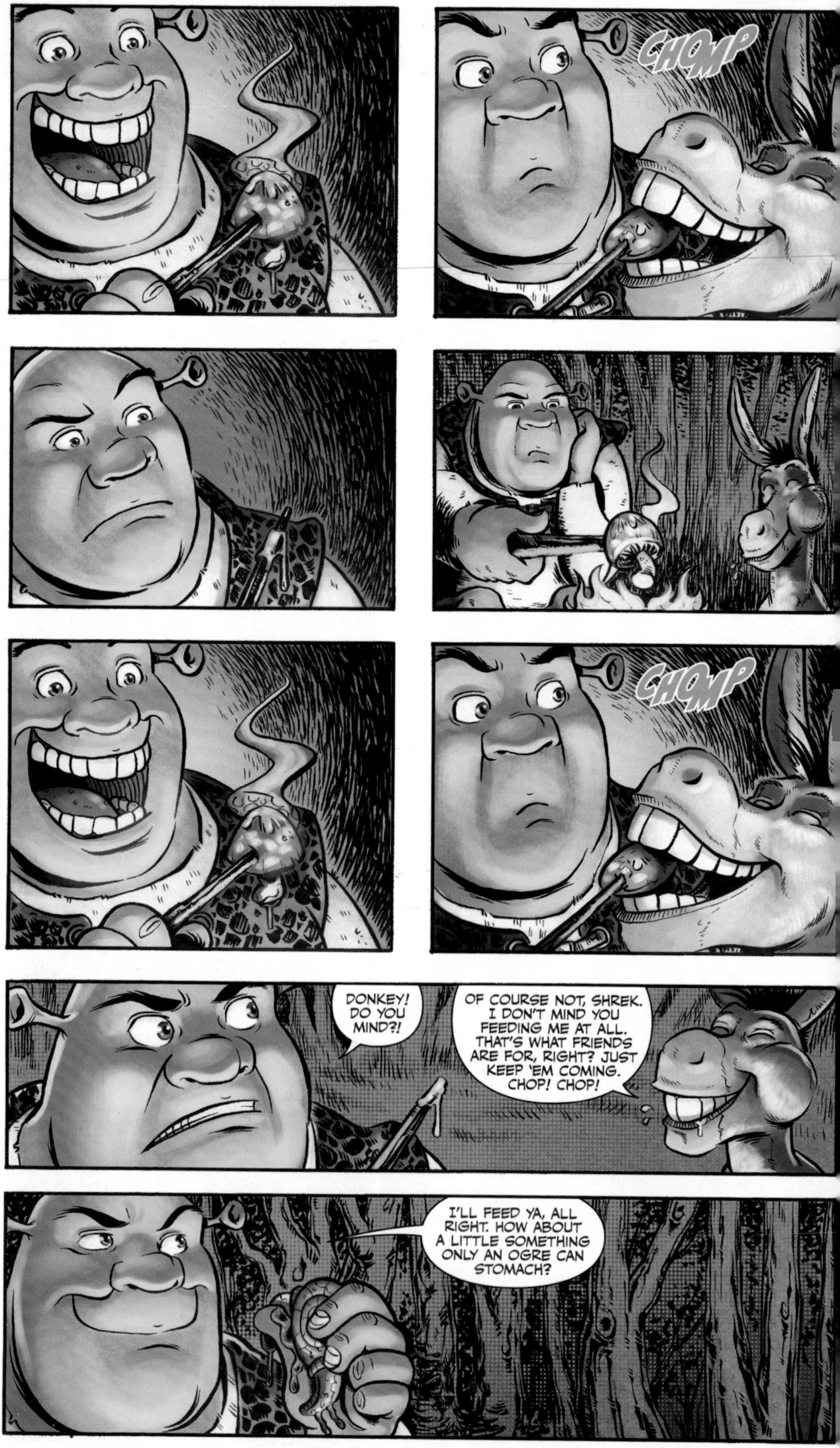
CHOMP
CHOMP
DONKEY! DO YOU MIND?!
OF COURSE NOT, SHREK. I DON'T MIND YOU FEEDING ME AT ALL. THAT'S WHAT FRIENDS ARE FOR, RIGHT? JUST KEEP 'EM COMING. CHOP! CHOP!
I'LL FEED YA, ALL RIGHT. HOW ABOUT A LITTLE SOMETHING ONLY AN OGRE CAN STOMACH?

MMMM. I CAN'T GET ENOUGH OF THESE TASTY LITTLE TREATS.

CRUNCH

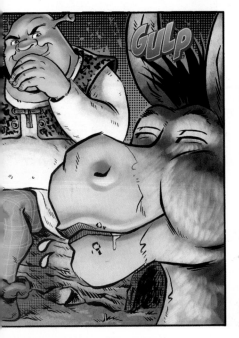

GULP

MMMM. TASTES LIKE CHICKEN.

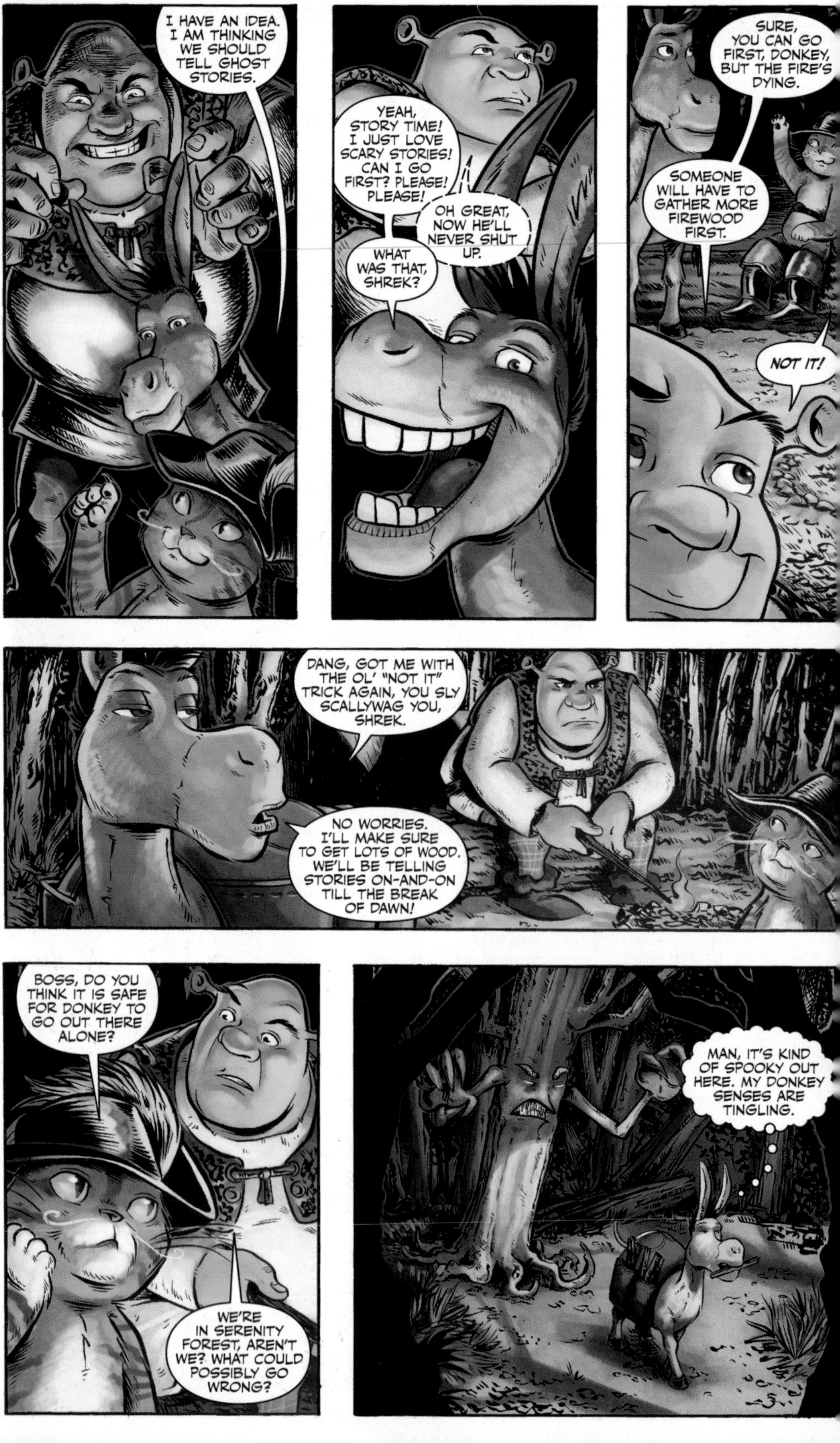
I HAVE AN IDEA. I AM THINKING WE SHOULD TELL GHOST STORIES.
YEAH, STORY TIME! I JUST LOVE SCARY STORIES! CAN I GO FIRST? PLEASE! PLEASE!
OH GREAT, NOW HE'LL NEVER SHUT UP.
WHAT WAS THAT, SHREK?
SURE, YOU CAN GO FIRST, DONKEY, BUT THE FIRE'S DYING.
SOMEONE WILL HAVE TO GATHER MORE FIREWOOD FIRST.
NOT IT!
DANG, GOT ME WITH THE OL' "NOT IT" TRICK AGAIN, YOU SLY SCALLYWAG YOU, SHREK.
NO WORRIES. I'LL MAKE SURE TO GET LOTS OF WOOD. WE'LL BE TELLING STORIES ON-AND-ON TILL THE BREAK OF DAWN!
BOSS, DO YOU THINK IT IS SAFE FOR DONKEY TO GO OUT THERE ALONE?
WE'RE IN SERENITY FOREST, AREN'T WE? WHAT COULD POSSIBLY GO WRONG?
MAN, IT'S KIND OF SPOOKY OUT HERE. MY DONKEY SENSES ARE TINGLING.

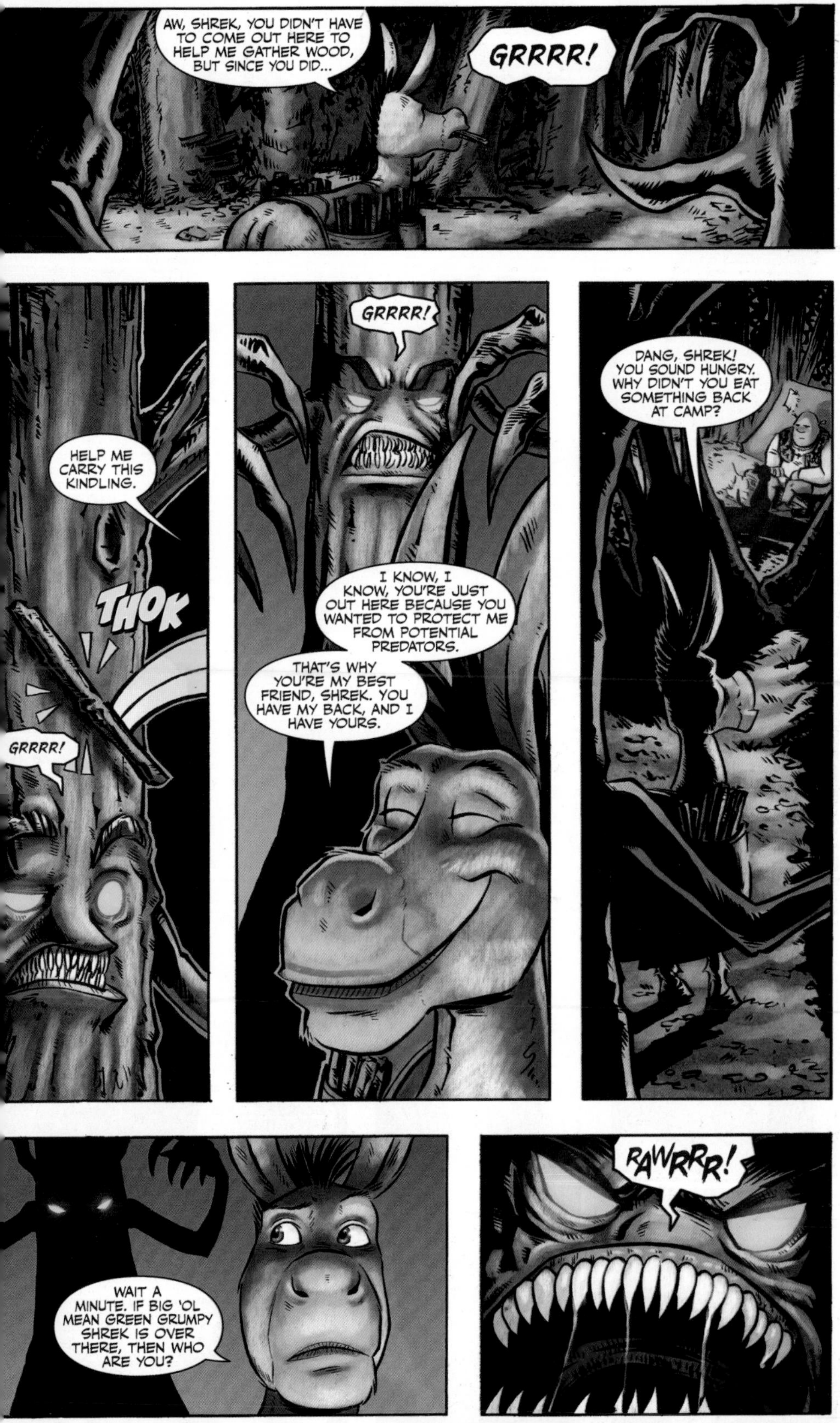
AW, SHREK, YOU DIDN'T HAVE TO COME OUT HERE TO HELP ME GATHER WOOD, BUT SINCE YOU DID...
GRRRR!
HELP ME CARRY THIS KINDLING.
THOK
GRRRR!
GRRRR!
I KNOW, I KNOW, YOU'RE JUST OUT HERE BECAUSE YOU WANTED TO PROTECT ME FROM POTENTIAL PREDATORS.
THAT'S WHY YOU'RE MY BEST FRIEND, SHREK. YOU HAVE MY BACK, AND I HAVE YOURS.
DANG, SHREK! YOU SOUND HUNGRY. WHY DIDN'T YOU EAT SOMETHING BACK AT CAMP?
WAIT A MINUTE. IF BIG 'OL MEAN GREEN GRUMPY SHREK IS OVER THERE, THEN WHO ARE YOU?
RAWRRR!

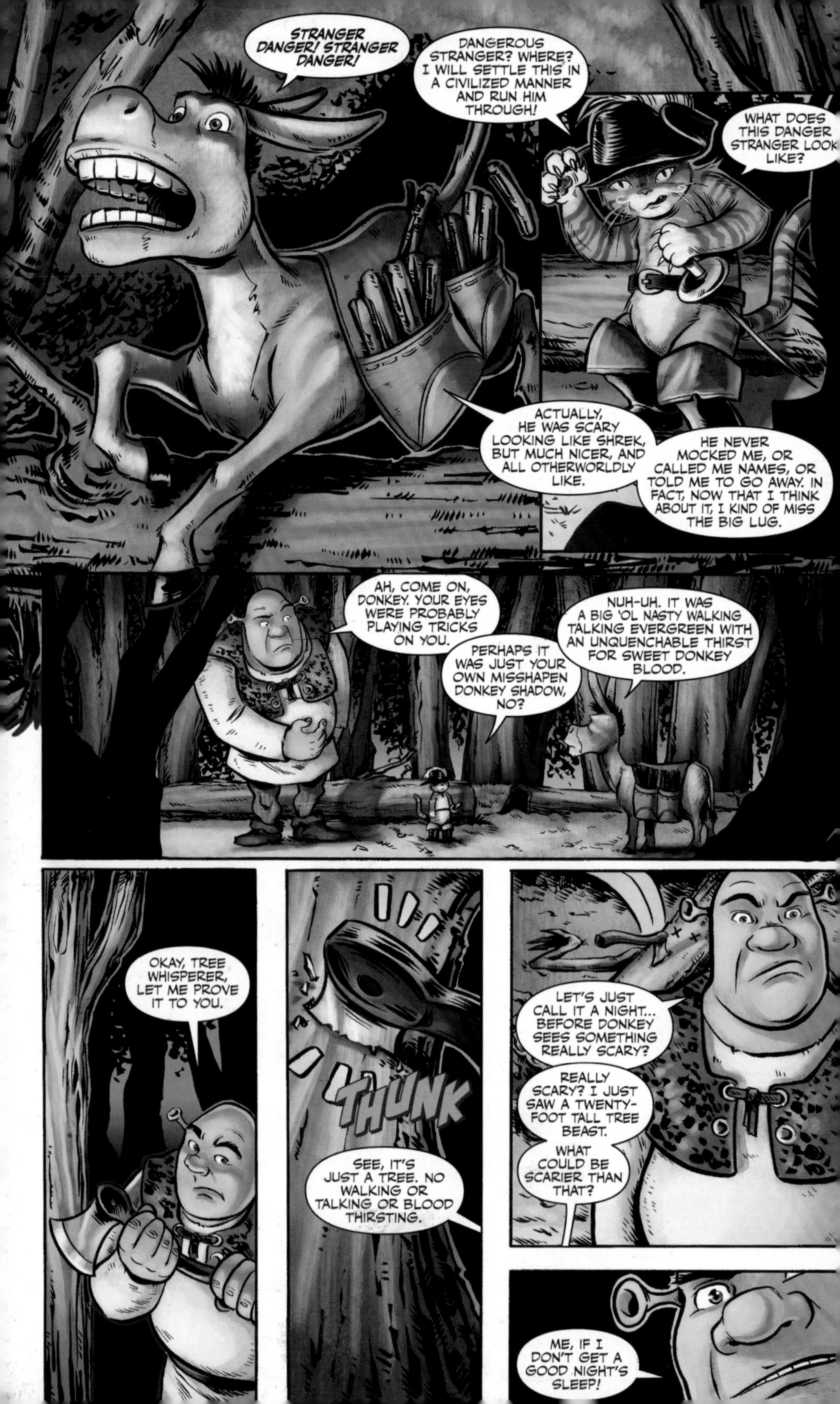

STRANGER DANGER! STRANGER DANGER!
DANGEROUS STRANGER? WHERE? I WILL SETTLE THIS IN A CIVILIZED MANNER AND RUN HIM THROUGH!
WHAT DOES THIS DANGER STRANGER LOOK LIKE?
ACTUALLY, HE WAS SCARY LOOKING LIKE SHREK, BUT MUCH NICER, AND ALL OTHERWORLDLY LIKE.
HE NEVER MOCKED ME, OR CALLED ME NAMES, OR TOLD ME TO GO AWAY. IN FACT, NOW THAT I THINK ABOUT IT, I KIND OF MISS THE BIG LUG.
AH, COME ON, DONKEY. YOUR EYES WERE PROBABLY PLAYING TRICKS ON YOU.
PERHAPS IT WAS JUST YOUR OWN MISSHAPEN DONKEY SHADOW, NO?
NUH-UH. IT WAS A BIG 'OL NASTY WALKING TALKING EVERGREEN WITH AN UNQUENCHABLE THIRST FOR SWEET DONKEY BLOOD.
OKAY, TREE WHISPERER, LET ME PROVE IT TO YOU.
THUNK
SEE, IT'S JUST A TREE. NO WALKING OR TALKING OR BLOOD THIRSTING.
LET'S JUST CALL IT A NIGHT... BEFORE DONKEY SEES SOMETHING REALLY SCARY?
REALLY SCARY? I JUST SAW A TWENTY-FOOT TALL TREE BEAST.
WHAT COULD BE SCARIER THAN THAT?
ME, IF I DON'T GET A GOOD NIGHT'S SLEEP!

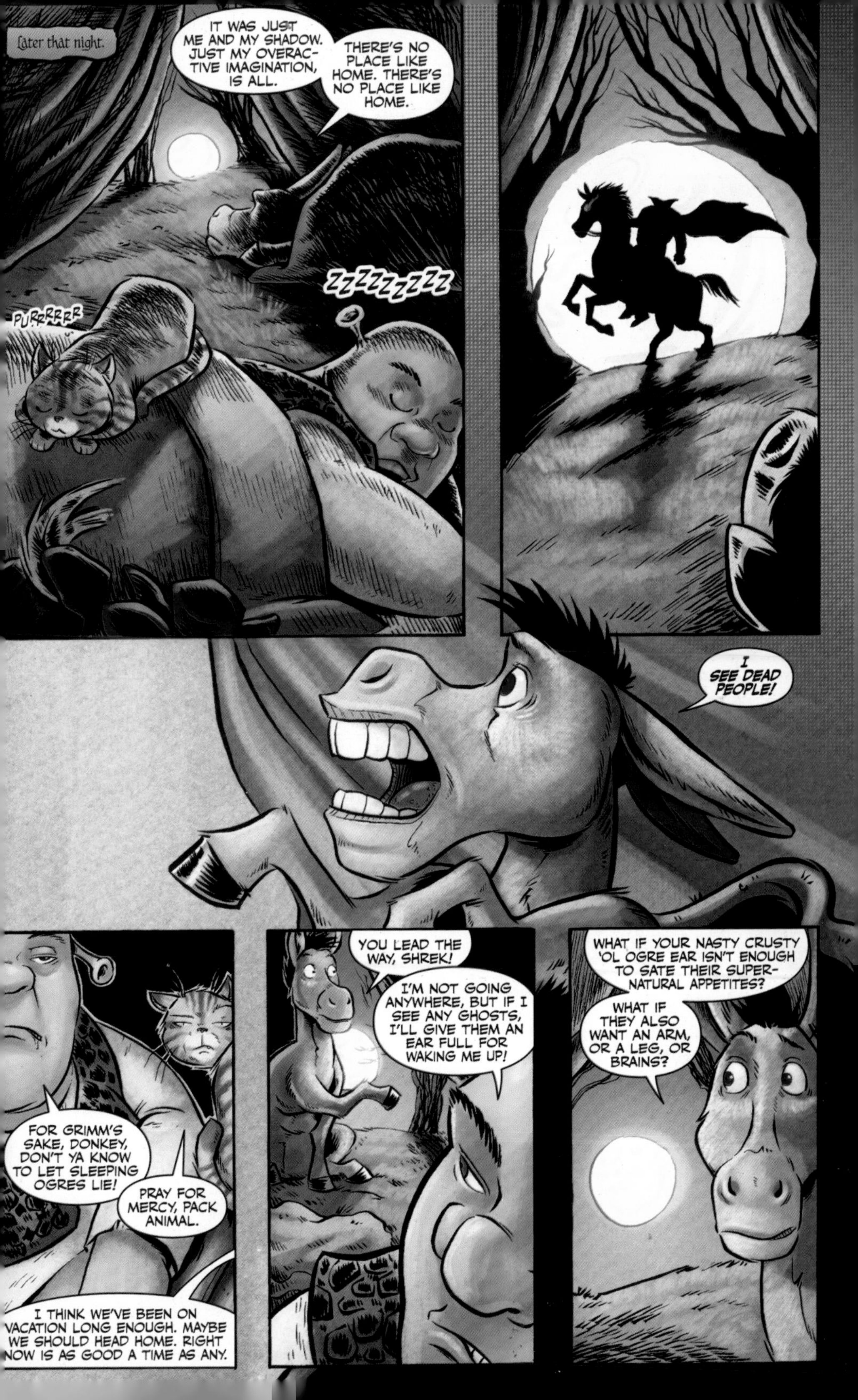
Later that night.
IT WAS JUST ME AND MY SHADOW. JUST MY OVERACTIVE IMAGINATION, IS ALL.
THERE'S NO PLACE LIKE HOME. THERE'S NO PLACE LIKE HOME.
PURRRRRR
ZZZZZZZZZ
I SEE DEAD PEOPLE!
FOR GRIMM'S SAKE, DONKEY, DON'T YA KNOW TO LET SLEEPING OGRES LIE!
PRAY FOR MERCY, PACK ANIMAL.
I THINK WE'VE BEEN ON VACATION LONG ENOUGH. MAYBE WE SHOULD HEAD HOME. RIGHT NOW IS AS GOOD A TIME AS ANY.
YOU LEAD THE WAY, SHREK!
I'M NOT GOING ANYWHERE, BUT IF I SEE ANY GHOSTS, I'LL GIVE THEM AN EAR FULL FOR WAKING ME UP!
WHAT IF YOUR NASTY CRUSTY 'OL OGRE EAR ISN'T ENOUGH TO SATE THEIR SUPER-NATURAL APPETITES?
WHAT IF THEY ALSO WANT AN ARM, OR A LEG, OR BRAINS?

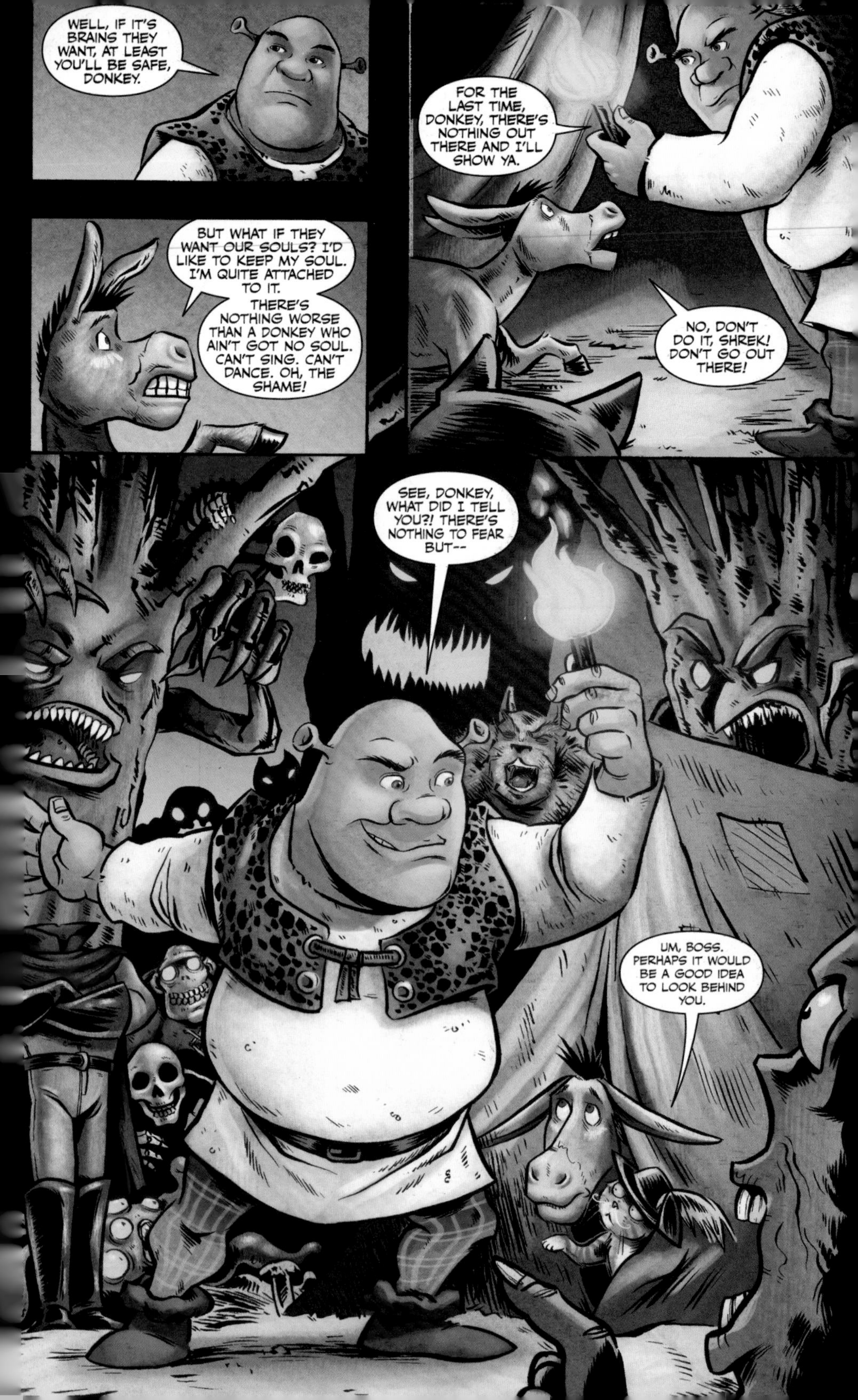
WELL, IF IT'S BRAINS THEY WANT, AT LEAST YOU'LL BE SAFE, DONKEY.
BUT WHAT IF THEY WANT OUR SOULS? I'D LIKE TO KEEP MY SOUL. I'M QUITE ATTACHED TO IT.
THERE'S NOTHING WORSE THAN A DONKEY WHO AIN'T GOT NO SOUL. CAN'T SING. CAN'T DANCE. OH, THE SHAME!
FOR THE LAST TIME, DONKEY, THERE'S NOTHING OUT THERE AND I'LL SHOW YA.
NO, DON'T DO IT, SHREK! DON'T GO OUT THERE!
SEE, DONKEY, WHAT DID I TELL YOU?! THERE'S NOTHING TO FEAR BUT--
UM, BOSS. PERHAPS IT WOULD BE A GOOD IDEA TO LOOK BEHIND YOU.

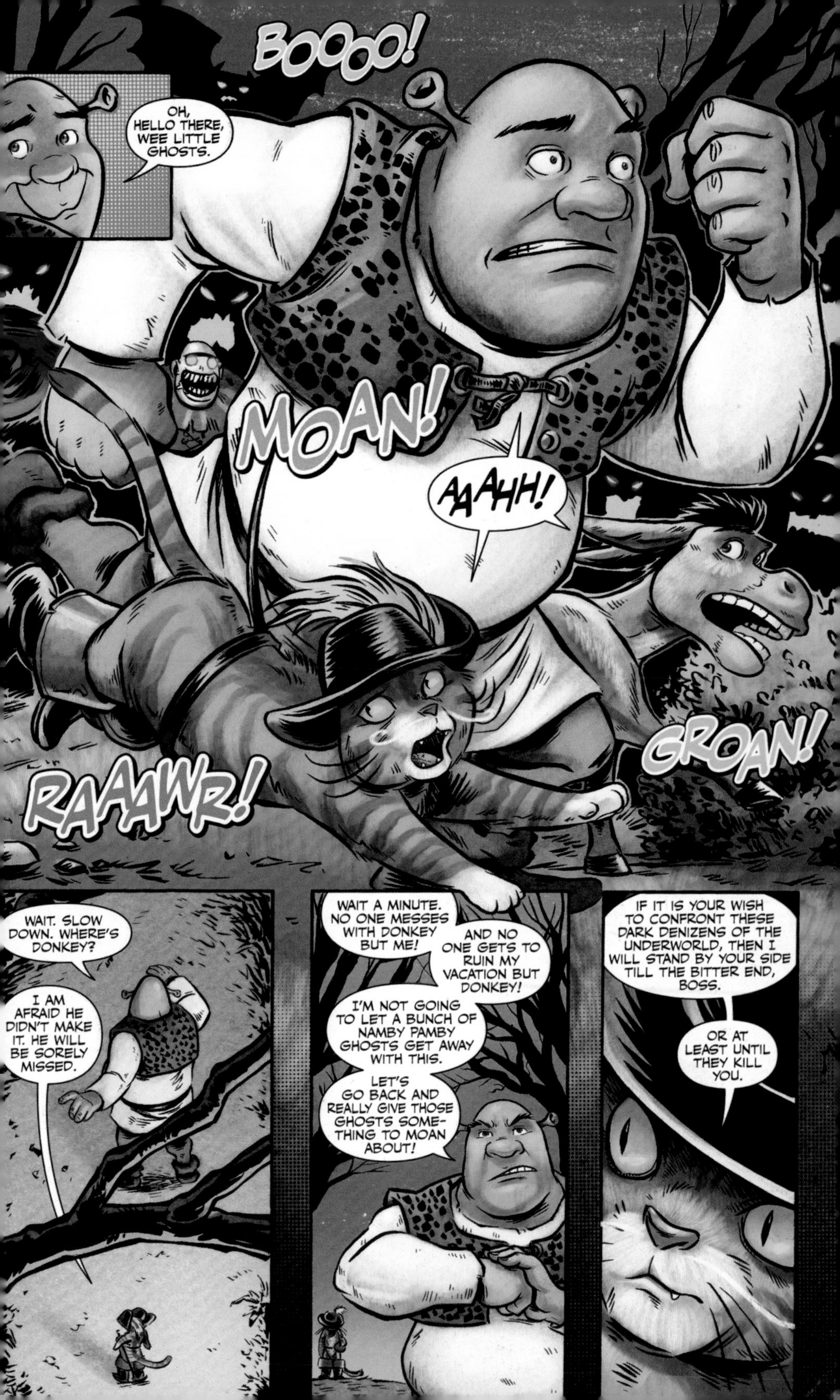
BOOOOO!
OH, HELLO THERE, WEE LITTLE GHOSTS.
MOAN!
AAAHH!
GROAN!
RAAAWR!
WAIT. SLOW DOWN. WHERE'S DONKEY?
I AM AFRAID HE DIDN'T MAKE IT. HE WILL BE SORELY MISSED.
WAIT A MINUTE. NO ONE MESSES WITH DONKEY BUT ME!
AND NO ONE GETS TO RUIN MY VACATION BUT DONKEY!
I'M NOT GOING TO LET A BUNCH OF NAMBY PAMBY GHOSTS GET AWAY WITH THIS.
LET'S GO BACK AND REALLY GIVE THOSE GHOSTS SOME-THING TO MOAN ABOUT!
IF IT IS YOUR WISH TO CONFRONT THESE DARK DENIZENS OF THE UNDERWORLD, THEN I WILL STAND BY YOUR SIDE TILL THE BITTER END, BOSS.
OR AT LEAST UNTIL THEY KILL YOU.

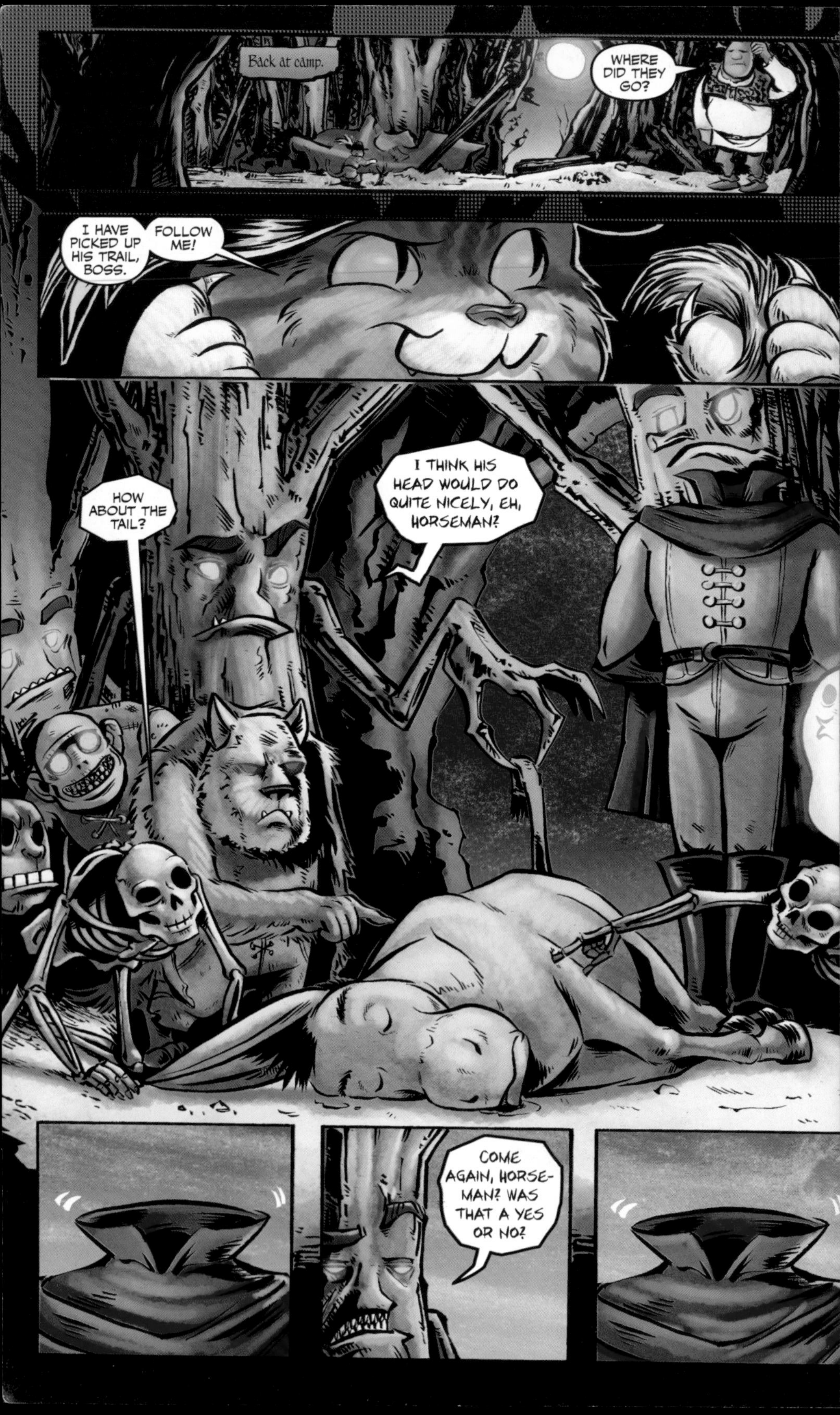
Back at camp.
WHERE DID THEY GO?
I HAVE PICKED UP HIS TRAIL, BOSS.
FOLLOW ME!
HOW ABOUT THE TAIL?
I THINK HIS HEAD WOULD DO QUITE NICELY, EH, HORSEMAN?
COME AGAIN, HORSE-MAN? WAS THAT A YES OR NO?

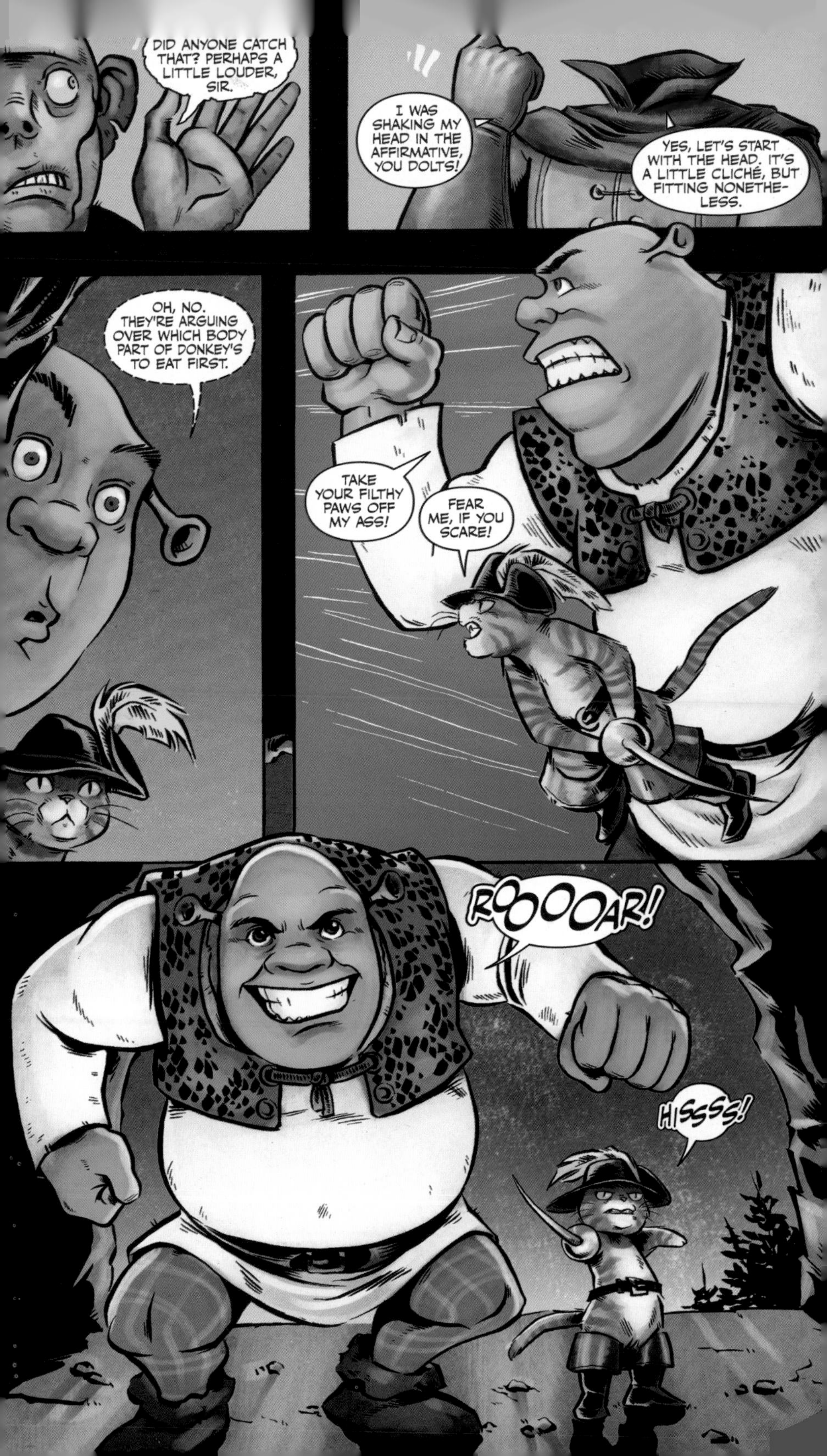
DID ANYONE CATCH THAT? PERHAPS A LITTLE LOUDER, SIR.
I WAS SHAKING MY HEAD IN THE AFFIRMATIVE, YOU DOLTS!
YES, LET'S START WITH THE HEAD. IT'S A LITTLE CLICHÉ, BUT FITTING NONETHELESS.
OH, NO. THEY'RE ARGUING OVER WHICH BODY PART OF DONKEY'S TO EAT FIRST.
TAKE YOUR FILTHY PAWS OFF MY ASS!
FEAR ME, IF YOU SCARE!
ROOOOAR!
HISSSS!

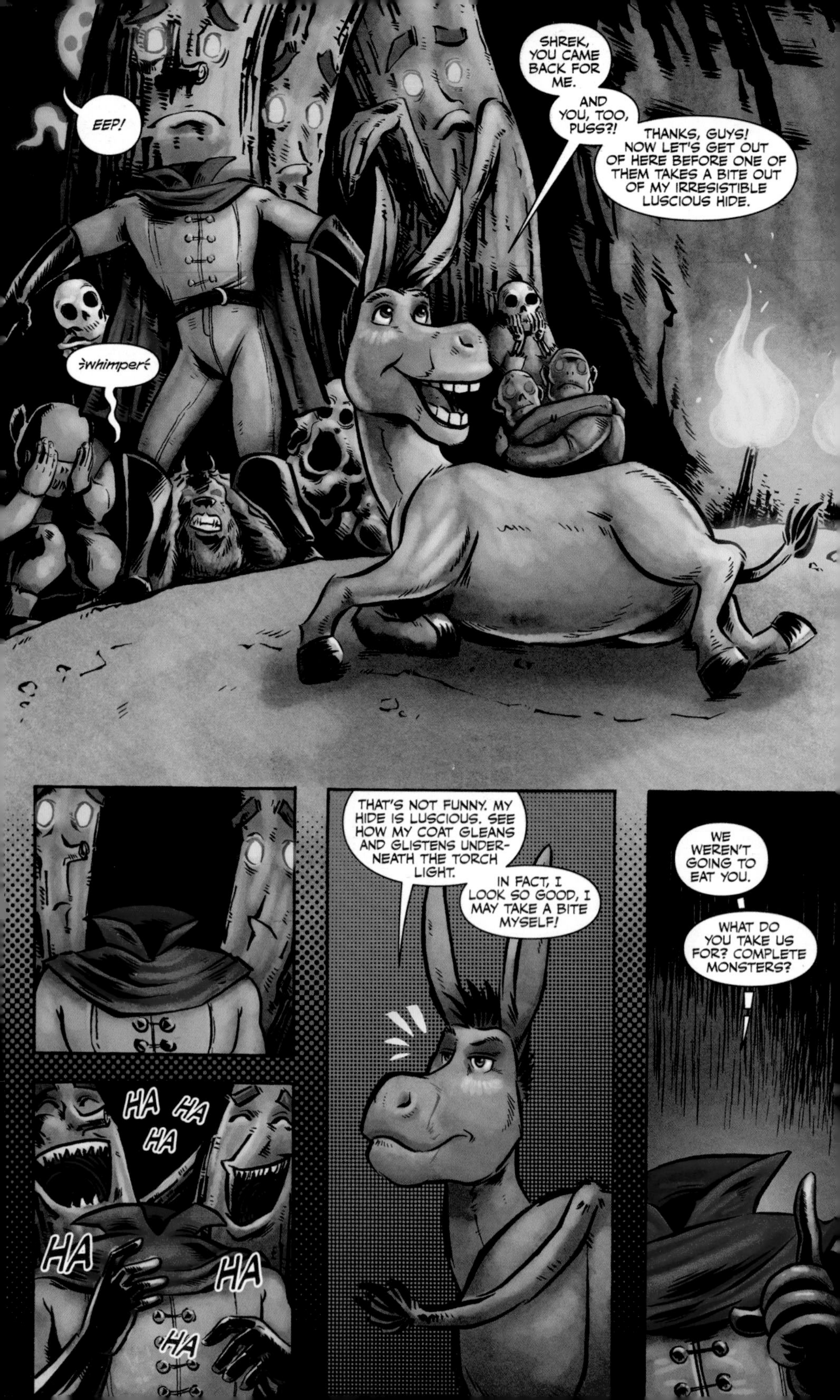

EEP!
SHREK, YOU CAME BACK FOR ME.
AND YOU, TOO, PUSS?!
THANKS, GUYS! NOW LET'S GET OUT OF HERE BEFORE ONE OF THEM TAKES A BITE OUT OF MY IRRESISTIBLE LUSCIOUS HIDE.
whimper
HA HA HA
HA HA HA
THAT'S NOT FUNNY. MY HIDE IS LUSCIOUS. SEE HOW MY COAT GLEANS AND GLISTENS UNDERNEATH THE TORCH LIGHT.
IN FACT, I LOOK SO GOOD, I MAY TAKE A BITE MYSELF!
WE WEREN'T GOING TO EAT YOU.
WHAT DO YOU TAKE US FOR? COMPLETE MONSTERS?

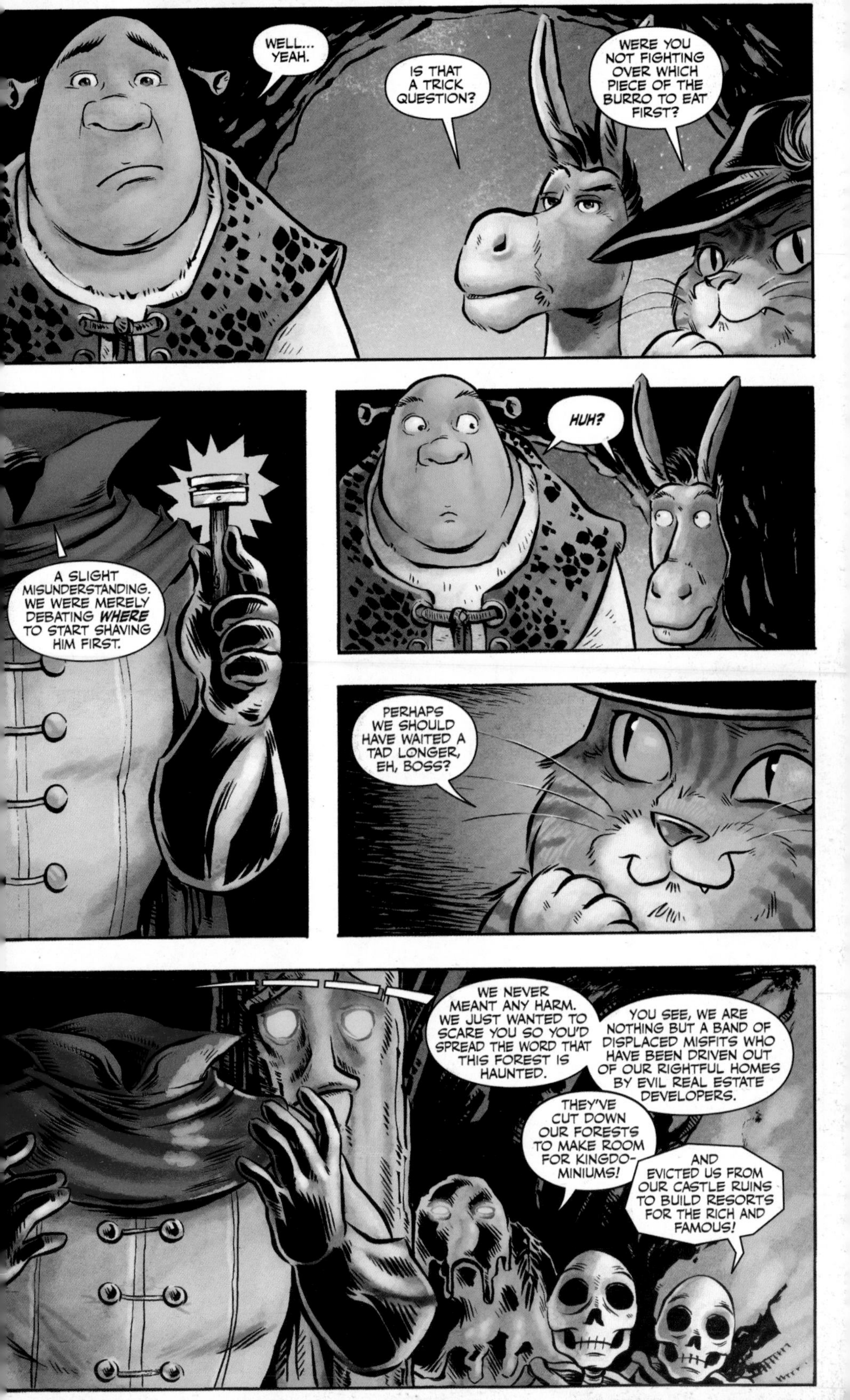

WELL... YEAH.
IS THAT A TRICK QUESTION?
WERE YOU NOT FIGHTING OVER WHICH PIECE OF THE BURRO TO EAT FIRST?
A SLIGHT MISUNDERSTANDING. WE WERE MERELY DEBATING WHERE TO START SHAVING HIM FIRST.
HUH?
PERHAPS WE SHOULD HAVE WAITED A TAD LONGER, EH, BOSS?
WE NEVER MEANT ANY HARM. WE JUST WANTED TO SCARE YOU SO YOU'D SPREAD THE WORD THAT THIS FOREST IS HAUNTED.
YOU SEE, WE ARE NOTHING BUT A BAND OF DISPLACED MISFITS WHO HAVE BEEN DRIVEN OUT OF OUR RIGHTFUL HOMES BY EVIL REAL ESTATE DEVELOPERS.
THEY'VE CUT DOWN OUR FORESTS TO MAKE ROOM FOR KINGDO-MINIUMS!
AND EVICTED US FROM OUR CASTLE RUINS TO BUILD RESORTS FOR THE RICH AND FAMOUS!

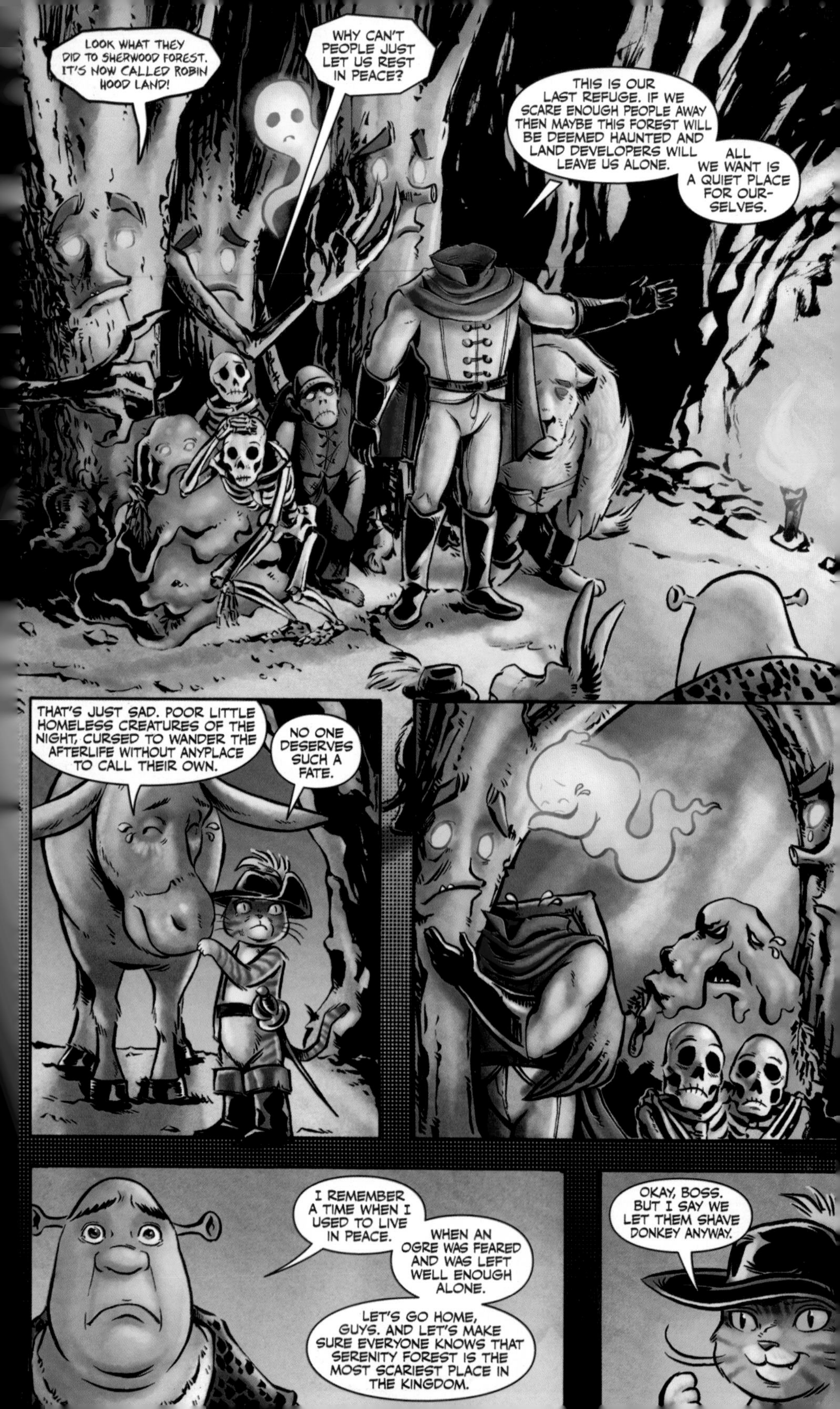

LOOK WHAT THEY DID TO SHERWOOD FOREST. IT'S NOW CALLED ROBIN HOOD LAND!
WHY CAN'T PEOPLE JUST LET US REST IN PEACE?
THIS IS OUR LAST REFUGE. IF WE SCARE ENOUGH PEOPLE AWAY THEN MAYBE THIS FOREST WILL BE DEEMED HAUNTED AND LAND DEVELOPERS WILL LEAVE US ALONE.
ALL WE WANT IS A QUIET PLACE FOR OUR-SELVES.
THAT'S JUST SAD. POOR LITTLE HOMELESS CREATURES OF THE NIGHT, CURSED TO WANDER THE AFTERLIFE WITHOUT ANYPLACE TO CALL THEIR OWN.
NO ONE DESERVES SUCH A FATE.
I REMEMBER A TIME WHEN I USED TO LIVE IN PEACE.
WHEN AN OGRE WAS FEARED AND WAS LEFT WELL ENOUGH ALONE.
LET'S GO HOME, GUYS. AND LET'S MAKE SURE EVERYONE KNOWS THAT SERENITY FOREST IS THE MOST SCARIEST PLACE IN THE KINGDOM.
OKAY, BOSS. BUT I SAY WE LET THEM SHAVE DONKEY ANYWAY.

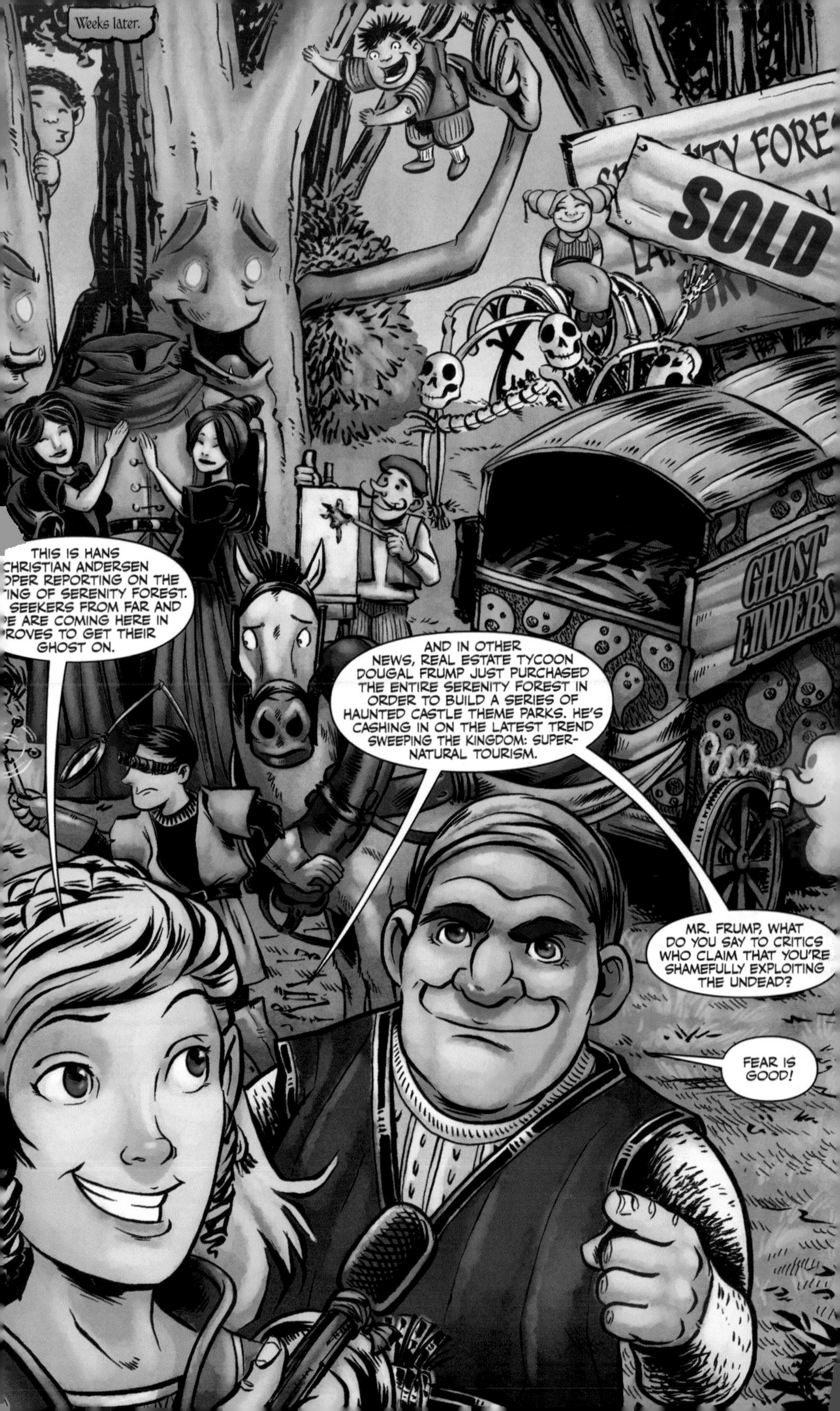

Weeks later.
SOLD
GHOST FINDERS
THIS IS HANS CHRISTIAN ANDERSEN
OPER REPORTING ON THE
TING OF SERENITY FOREST.
SEEKERS FROM FAR AND
E ARE COMING HERE IN
ROVES TO GET THEIR
GHOST ON.
AND IN OTHER NEWS, REAL ESTATE TYCOON DOUGAL FRUMP JUST PURCHASED THE ENTIRE SERENITY FOREST IN ORDER TO BUILD A SERIES OF HAUNTED CASTLE THEME PARKS. HE'S CASHING IN ON THE LATEST TREND SWEEPING THE KINGDOM: SUPER-NATURAL TOURISM.
MR. FRUMP, WHAT DO YOU SAY TO CRITICS WHO CLAIM THAT YOU'RE SHAMEFULLY EXPLOITING THE UNDEAD?
FEAR IS GOOD!

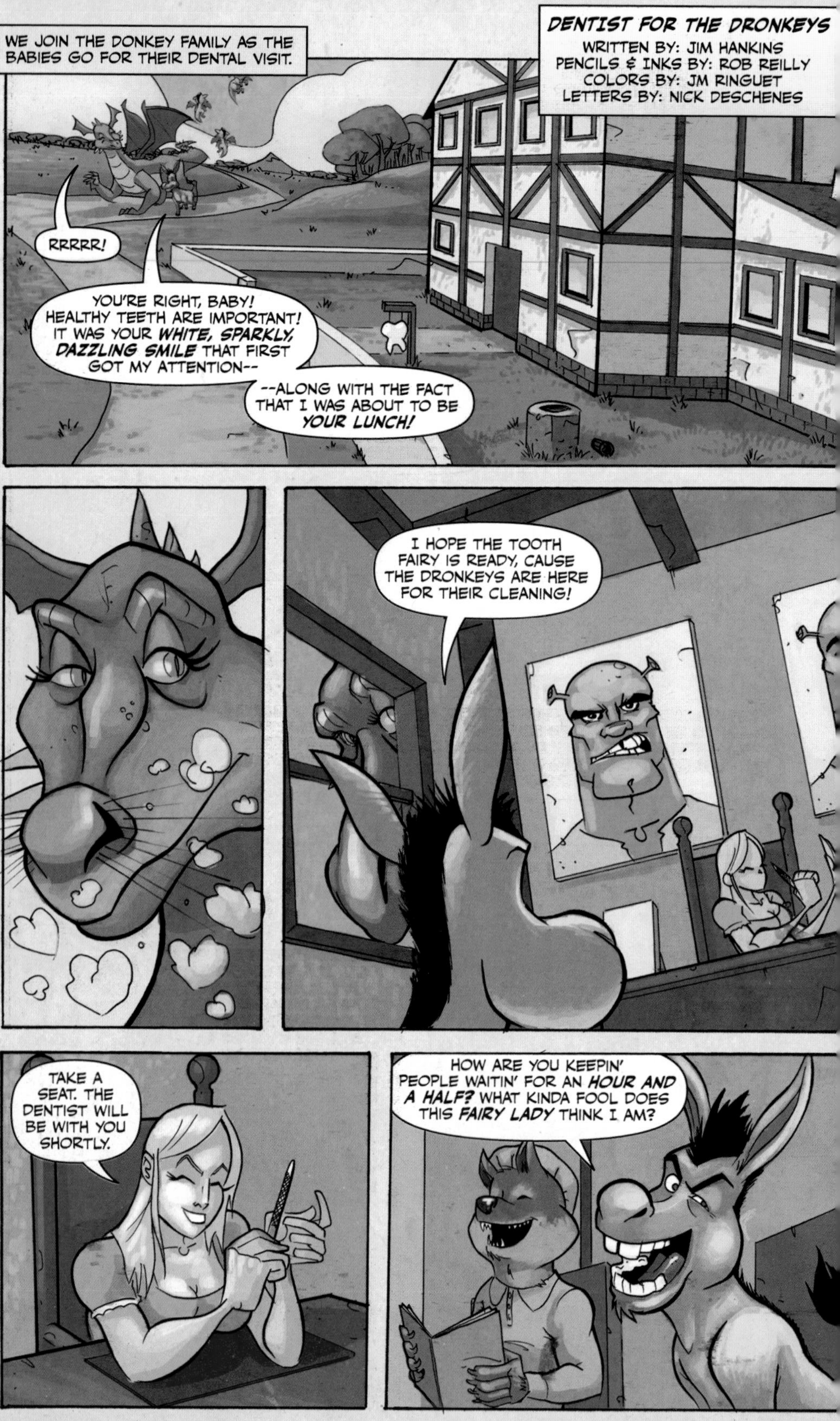
WE JOIN THE DONKEY FAMILY AS THE BABIES GO FOR THEIR DENTAL VISIT.
DENTIST FOR THE DRONKEYS
WRITTEN BY: JIM HANKINS
PENCILS & INKS BY: ROB REILLY
COLORS BY: JM RINGUET
LETTERS BY: NICK DESCHENES
RRRRR!
YOU'RE RIGHT, BABY! HEALTHY TEETH ARE IMPORTANT! IT WAS YOUR WHITE, SPARKLY, DAZZLING SMILE THAT FIRST GOT MY ATTENTION--
--ALONG WITH THE FACT THAT I WAS ABOUT TO BE YOUR LUNCH!
I HOPE THE TOOTH FAIRY IS READY, CAUSE THE DRONKEYS ARE HERE FOR THEIR CLEANING!
TAKE A SEAT. THE DENTIST WILL BE WITH YOU SHORTLY.
HOW ARE YOU KEEPIN' PEOPLE WAITIN' FOR AN HOUR AND A HALF? WHAT KINDA FOOL DOES THIS FAIRY LADY THINK I AM?

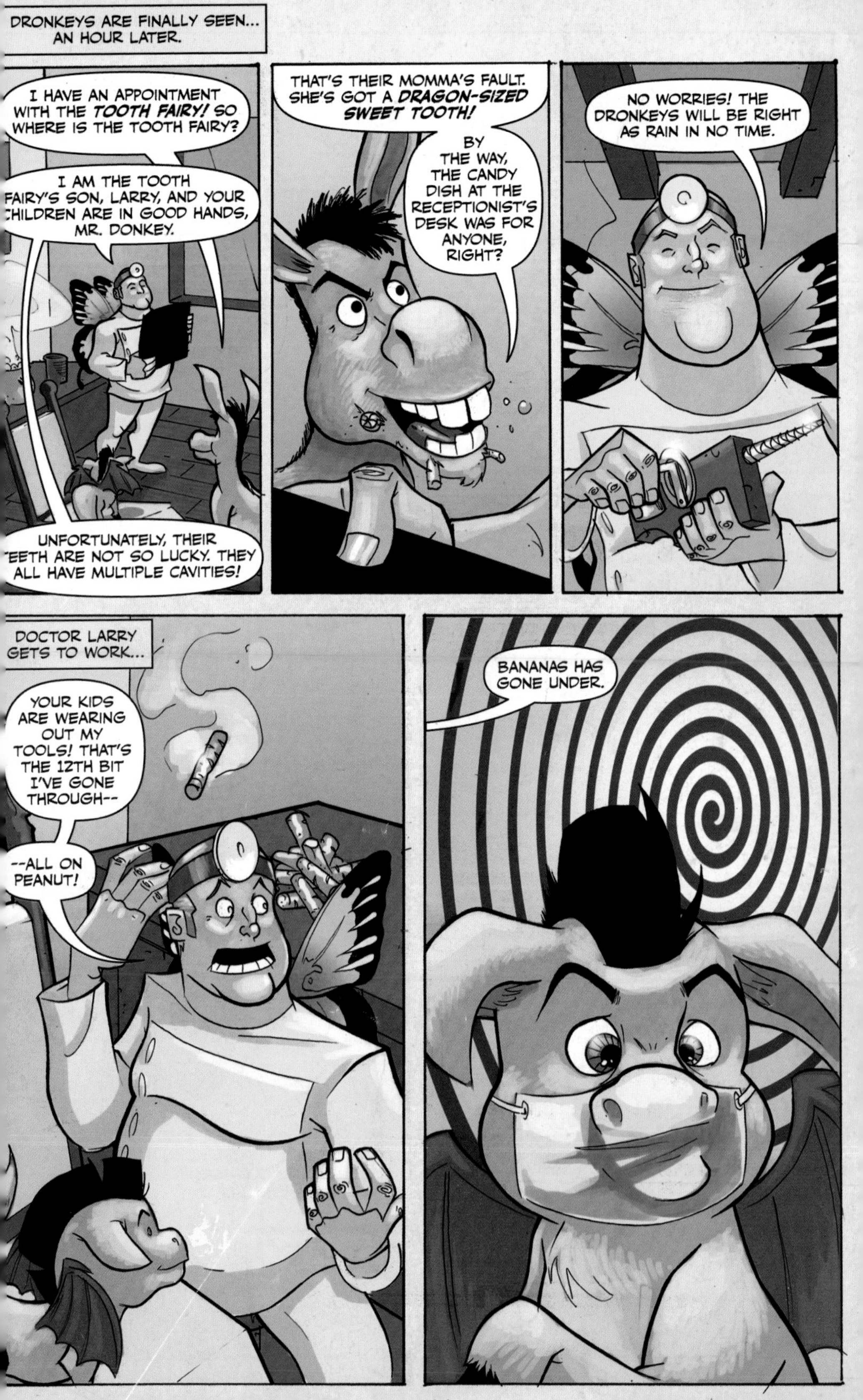
DRONKEYS ARE FINALLY SEEN... AN HOUR LATER.
I HAVE AN APPOINTMENT WITH THE *TOOTH FAIRY!* SO WHERE IS THE TOOTH FAIRY?
I AM THE TOOTH FAIRY'S SON, LARRY, AND YOUR CHILDREN ARE IN GOOD HANDS, MR. DONKEY.
UNFORTUNATELY, THEIR TEETH ARE NOT SO LUCKY. THEY ALL HAVE MULTIPLE CAVITIES!
THAT'S THEIR MOMMA'S FAULT. SHE'S GOT A *DRAGON-SIZED SWEET TOOTH!*
BY THE WAY, THE CANDY DISH AT THE RECEPTIONIST'S DESK WAS FOR ANYONE, RIGHT?
NO WORRIES! THE DRONKEYS WILL BE RIGHT AS RAIN IN NO TIME.
DOCTOR LARRY GETS TO WORK...
YOUR KIDS ARE WEARING OUT MY TOOLS! THAT'S THE 12TH BIT I'VE GONE THROUGH--
--ALL ON PEANUT!
BANANAS HAS GONE UNDER.

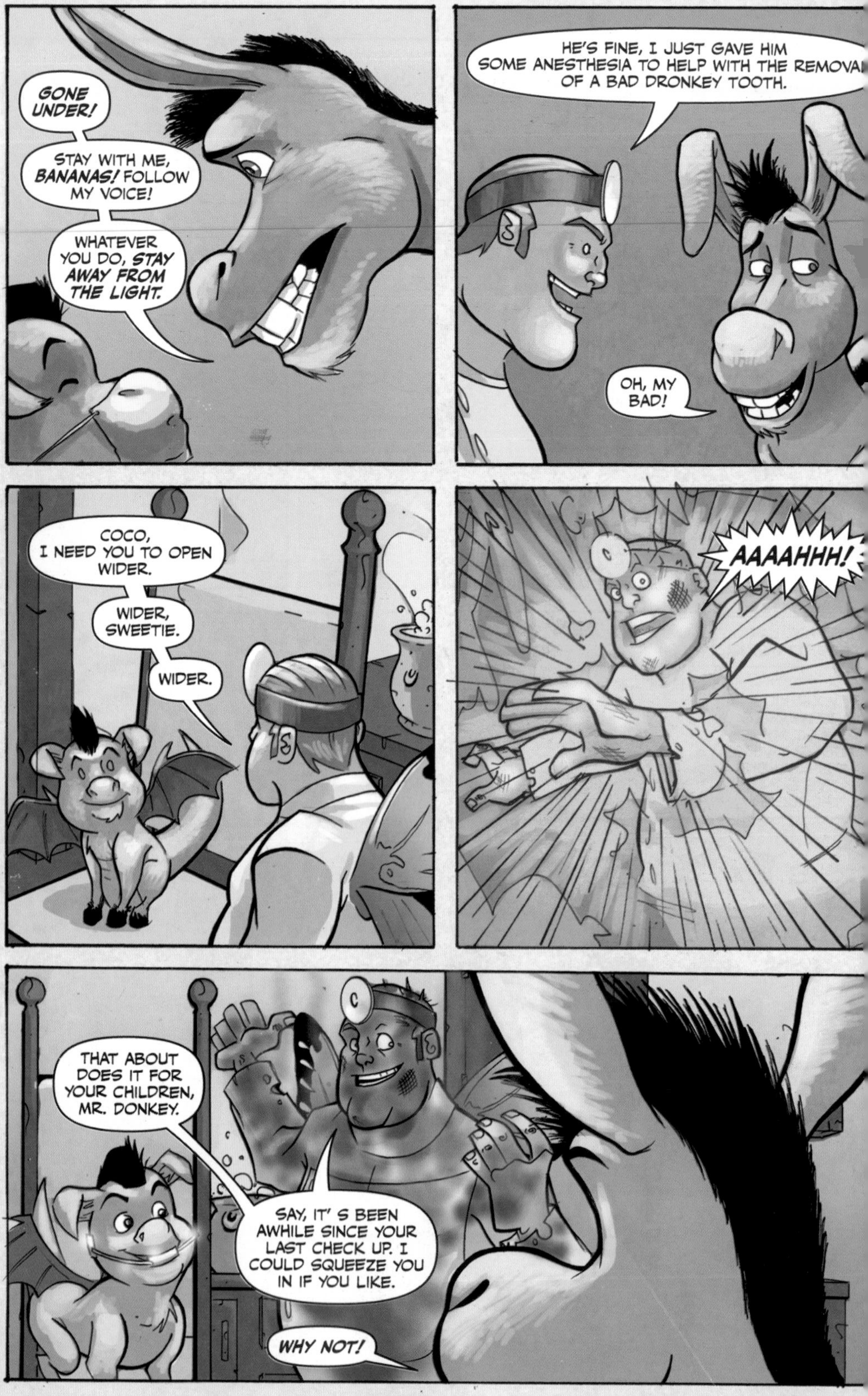

GONE UNDER!
STAY WITH ME, BANANAS! FOLLOW MY VOICE!
WHATEVER YOU DO, STAY AWAY FROM THE LIGHT.
HE'S FINE, I JUST GAVE HIM SOME ANESTHESIA TO HELP WITH THE REMOVAL OF A BAD DRONKEY TOOTH.
OH, MY BAD!
COCO, I NEED YOU TO OPEN WIDER.
WIDER, SWEETIE.
WIDER.
AAAAHHH!
THAT ABOUT DOES IT FOR YOUR CHILDREN, MR. DONKEY.
SAY, IT' S BEEN AWHILE SINCE YOUR LAST CHECK UP. I COULD SQUEEZE YOU IN IF YOU LIKE.
WHY NOT!

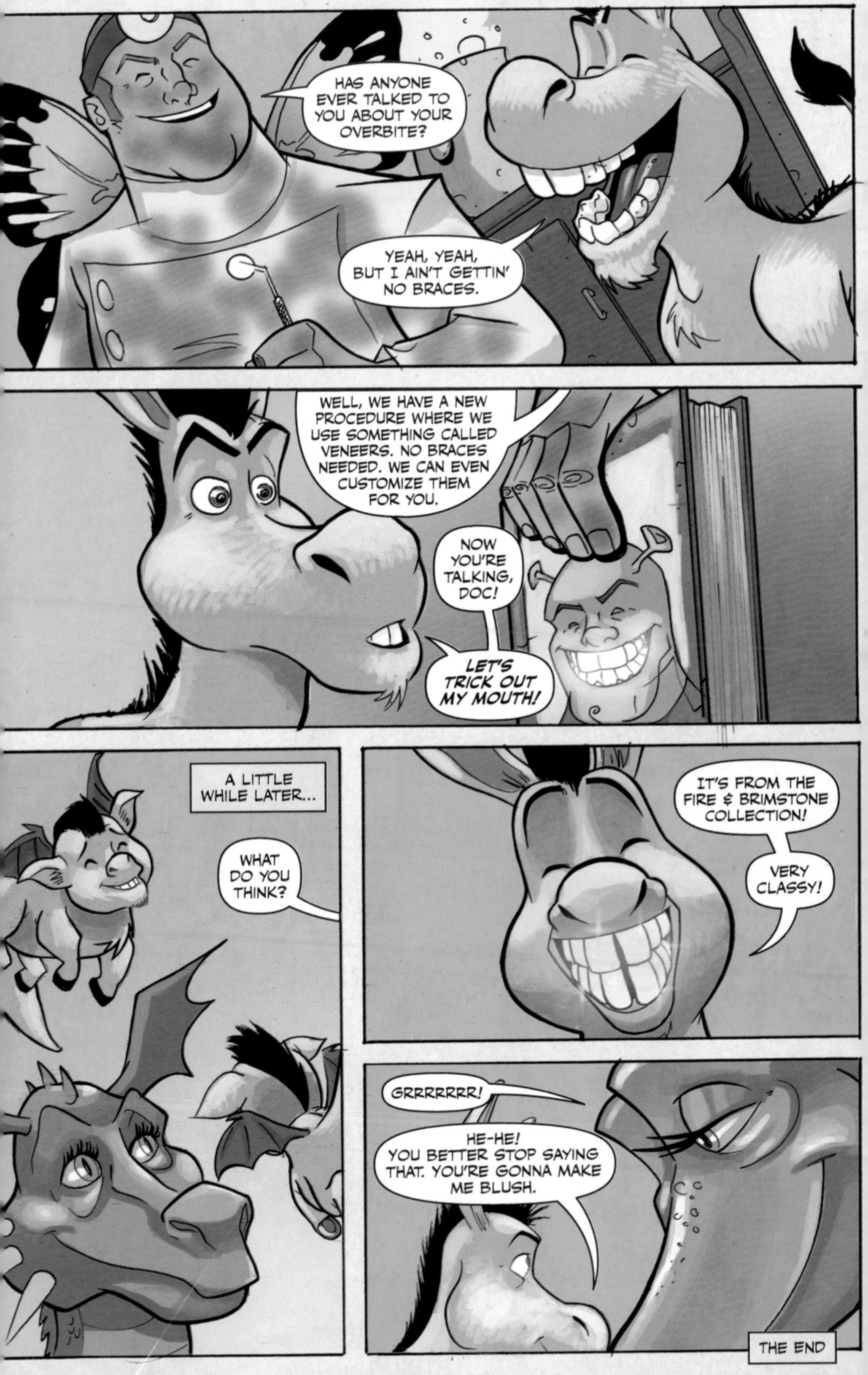
HAS ANYONE EVER TALKED TO YOU ABOUT YOUR OVERBITE?
YEAH, YEAH, BUT I AIN'T GETTIN' NO BRACES.
WELL, WE HAVE A NEW PROCEDURE WHERE WE USE SOMETHING CALLED VENEERS. NO BRACES NEEDED. WE CAN EVEN CUSTOMIZE THEM FOR YOU.
NOW YOU'RE TALKING, DOC!
LET'S TRICK OUT MY MOUTH!
A LITTLE WHILE LATER...
WHAT DO YOU THINK?
IT'S FROM THE FIRE & BRIMSTONE COLLECTION!
VERY CLASSY!
GRRRRRRR!
HE-HE! YOU BETTER STOP SAYING THAT. YOU'RE GONNA MAKE ME BLUSH.
THE END

OPERATION: *Read Comics* is a go!

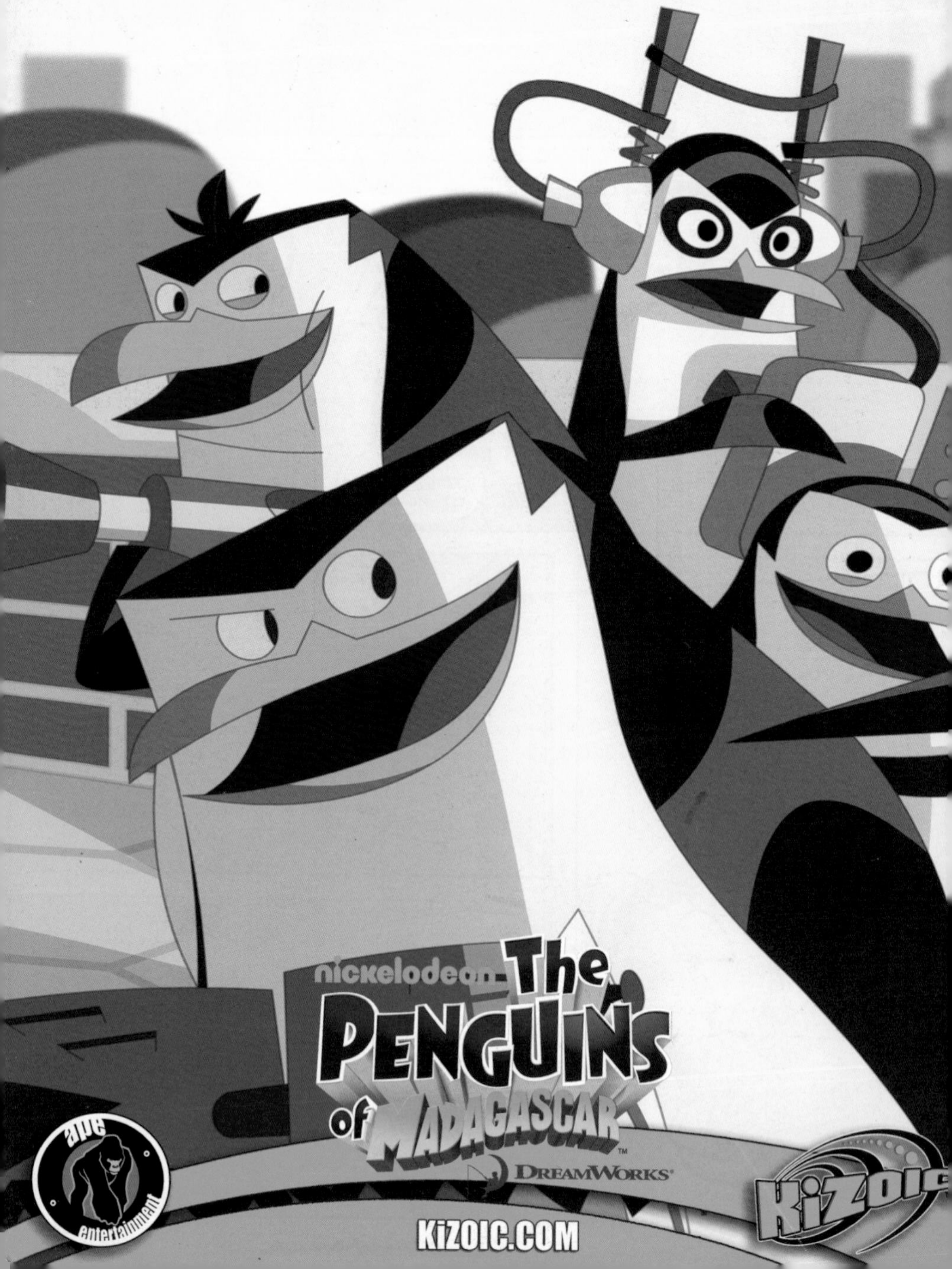
nickelodeon
The PENGUINS of MADAGASCAR
DREAMWORKS
ape entertainment
KiZOIC
KIZOIC.COM

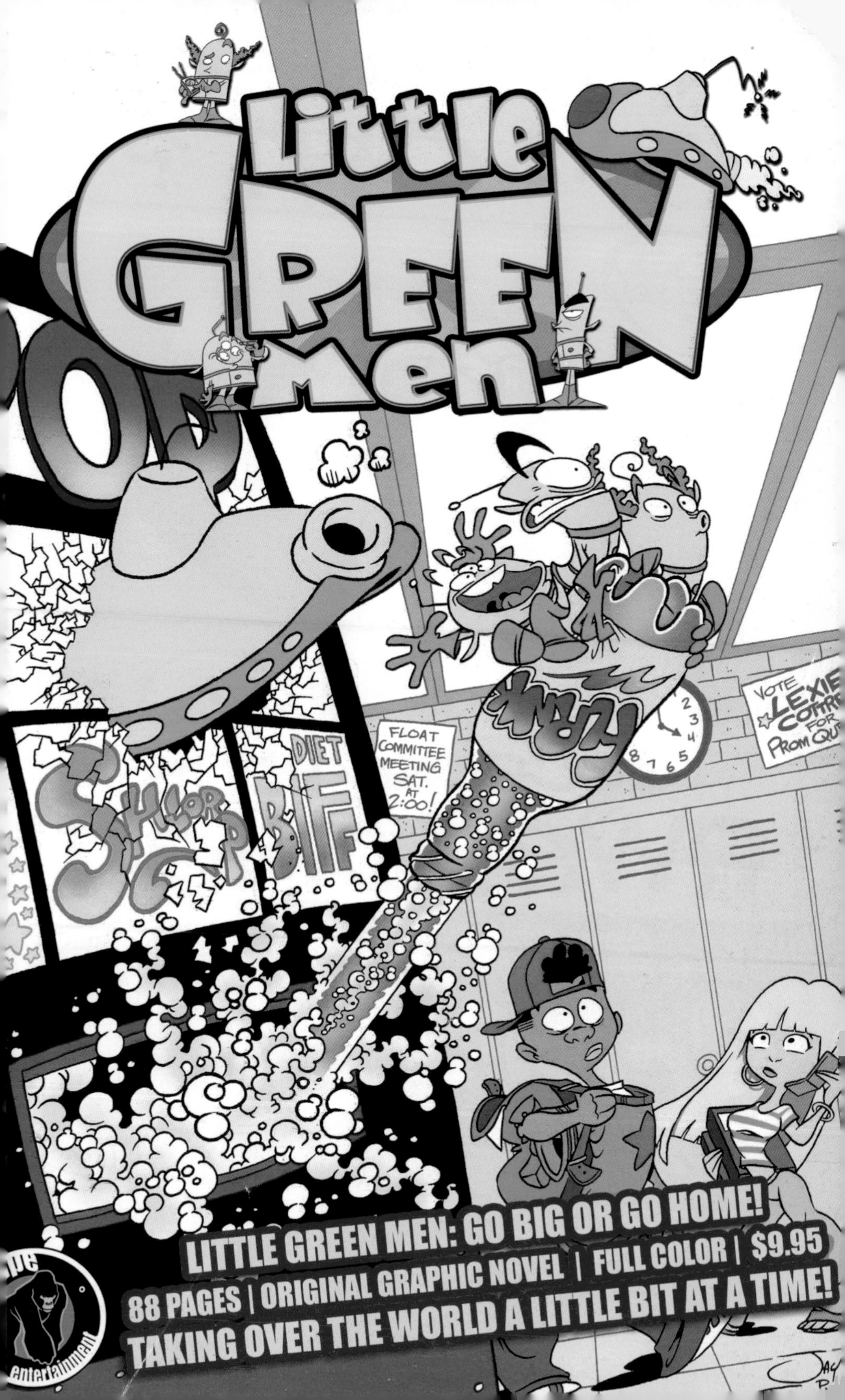
Little GREEN Men
FLOAT COMMITTEE MEETING SAT. AT 2:00!
DIET BIFF
LITTLE GREEN MEN: GO BIG OR GO HOME!
88 PAGES | ORIGINAL GRAPHIC NOVEL | FULL COLOR | $9.95
TAKING OVER THE WORLD A LITTLE BIT AT A TIME!